I was about to
that led to the b
sound. It was th
beating against
slowly up the tra            twenty feet,
then I saw Jessie.

She was standing two steps from the edge
of the cliff, gazing out at the ocean. Her
arms were outstretched and her nightgown
billowed behind her as it filled with the breeze
from off the water. Her eyes seemed fixed on
a point far out in the sea.

She took a step forward without looking
down, as if in a trance. One more step and
she would plunge over the edge.

**Books by Glen Ebisch**
*Lou Dunlop: Private Eye*
*Lou Dunlop: Cliffhanger*

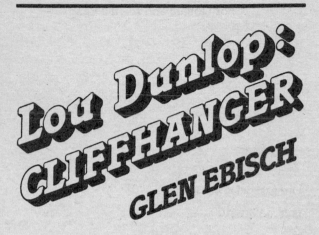

# Lou Dunlop: CLIFFHANGER

## GLEN EBISCH

CROSSWINDS

New York • Toronto
Sydney • Auckland
Manila

For Donald and Lucille Egan

First publication July 1987

ISBN 0-373-98004-3

**GLEN EBISCH** received his Ph.D. in philosophy from Columbia University and currently teaches at Elms College in Chicopee, Massachusetts. He is the author of a number of academic articles and a short story for young adults. In his fiction, he admits to being influenced by the works of Dashiell Hammett and Raymond Chandler. He frequently spends his summers admiring the Victorian houses in Cape May, New Jersey. His hobbies include reading, jogging and basketball.

# Chapter One

I wished the old yellow Volkswagen were a convertible, so we could put the top down and have the sun on our shoulders and the wind in our hair like they do in the movies. But since it would take a blowtorch and a hacksaw to turn the sedan into a convertible, and I didn't have either one with me, I decided to sit back and enjoy what I did have: a beautiful day, a beautiful girl and two beautiful weeks on beautiful Cape Cod. Everything was just beautiful.

I turned to Jessie and smiled. It must have been a silly, happy smile because she laughed a little in surprise and then smiled back.

"This is the life, Jes, the sun and the water, and nothing to do but enjoy them." I was really bubbling over.

"I'm glad you could come along. I really didn't think your father would let you. Didn't he say he wanted you to work all summer?"

I had been pretty amazed myself that he let me go, but I wasn't going to let on to Jessie.

"Well, I just convinced him that a guy needed a break before starting his senior year in high school, so it was either this or I was going to hop on the next freight train south."

"I'll bet that scared him. At the speed most of the trains around here move, school would be starting before you got out of the state. After all, it's only three weeks until the Dreaded Day."

"Yeah, but don't forget, we've got two weeks to drown ourselves in pleasure before then."

"Drown might be an unfortunate expression at the seashore, but I see your point."

Jessie went back to concentrating on the road, but I continued to look at her out of the corner of my eye, admiring her figure in the red tank top and cut-off jeans. That, and the blond hair, and the tan she had gotten over the summer, made her look sexy. Sexy, but at the same time wholesome, if you get what I mean. In the six months I had known her, the wild lipstick and the crazy clothes she used to wear had disappeared, and she seemed more relaxed. Like she didn't have to prove anything anymore.

"Where did your folks go in Europe?" I asked, shifting the position of my legs. We both had the front seats of the little car pushed all the way back, but with my thin six-foot-one body I still had to bend my knees to fit. For Jessie, who was a few inches shorter, it was just right. In high heels she would be almost my height. We'd never been out on that kind of fancy date, but I knew she would be perfect.

"To France. I think they were going to Paris and then somewhere along the southern coast," she replied.

"Did your brother go, too?"

"Yeah, they picked him up at college. He was taking some summer course that just ended. With his ulcer he probably needed the rest."

"Why didn't you go along?"

"I've seen France, and I really wanted to visit my aunt and uncle."

I swallowed hard. Every once in a while I forgot the differences between Jessie and me, and then they would come rushing back. Her family was pretty well off, and they did those little things like travel and eat in expensive restaurants that my father, who's a cop, and I can't afford to do. The farthest north I'd ever been was to Montreal and the farthest south was New York City, and both times we drove. I've never even been in an airplane. Seventeen and never been off the ground. Sometimes it's hard to keep your self-respect.

"I hope you like my aunt and uncle," Jessie continued. "Aunt Millie can be a little vague sometimes, not quite with it, you know. But she really is nice. And Uncle Stephen isn't exactly my uncle, he's my stepuncle. He married Aunt Millie about seven years ago after Uncle Walter died of a heart attack. He's a psychiatrist, but I think you'll like him too."

"A psychiatrist! I guess I'll have to be careful about what I say, or he'll find out about my hidden desires," I said, giving Jessie a big leer.

She tried to look scared but ended up grinning. "He's not like that, but my cousin Molly will keep you jumping. She's only twelve but almost a genius."

"You said something the other day about another cousin who's in college."

"Yeah, that's David; he just graduated from college out in California. This is the first time he's been home in a long time. I'm really looking forward to seeing him," she gushed.

"Do you know him well?" I asked cautiously.

"I haven't seen him in four years, but when I was thirteen and he had just graduated from high school, I spent a whole summer out here. David and I went everywhere together and did everything."

Obviously here was the fly in the ointment, the snake in the grass, the worm in the apple. Some bronzed and beautiful college guy was going to whisk Jessie off for God knows what, while I would be stuck on the beach doing differential equations with some pint-size genius.

"I think you and David will really like each other," said Jessie, unknowingly turning the knife.

"Sure," I said with a touch of sarcasm. This guy could be a saint, but I already knew I would hate him.

"Besides you, he's my only real male friend, you know. I'd be really upset if the two of you didn't get along."

It sounded like a request, so I forced a smile. "I'm sure we'll get along just fine." But only if this guy turns out to be five feet tall and pimply, I said to myself.

We continued along Route 6. After we passed the exit for Orleans, the traffic thinned out, and fifteen minutes later we turned off the highway. Jessie took a couple more turns without glancing at Aunt Millie's hand-drawn map that I was holding on my lap. Finally we went up a short hill and started riding along the top of the ridge. On the left side was an ocean of sand formed into rolling dunes like dingy white waves. A few scraggly bushes grew between the hills, and once in a while you'd see an old house that looked as though it hadn't been lived in for years.

On the right side, there were higher dunes with lots of gray shingled houses playing hide-and-seek between them. Somehow you could tell by the color of the sky in the distance that somewhere out there, not too far away, was what we had traveled to see—the ocean.

Jessie made a quick right turn onto a street named Seagull Lane. There was so much sand on the road that the blacktop was only a narrow strip down the center. We followed this line for about fifty yards and then swung into the driveway of a two-story house, which, of course, had gray shingles.

"Well, this is it!" shouted Jessie, flinging open the door and jumping out. "Isn't it wonderful? Smell the sea and feel that breeze!"

I got out and sure enough, there was a breeze, more like a warm wind in fact, and on it you could almost taste the salt. There was a smell, too, partly of salt, but partly that kind of hard to describe aroma I'd smelled once before when I'd accidentally left a piece of flounder in the bottom of the grocery bag for a week.

"Jessie?" a thin, middle-aged woman asked as she pushed open the side screen door. She looked at Jessie as though trying to remember something, then smiled. "Well, you have changed, but I'd still know you anywhere. And I think you're even prettier than I remembered you being." They hugged and Jessie introduced me.

"Hello, Louis, I'm glad you were able to come."

"So am I, Mrs. Marshal. This is certainly a wonderful spot."

"Yes, I guess it is," she replied slowly, as though thinking about it for the first time. "From the second floor you can look quite far out to sea. On a clear day it's a splendid sight."

We pulled our bags out of the trunk and followed her into the house. In spite of the old-looking gray shingles, the inside of the place seemed new. Aunt Millie led us through a large kitchen with a dishwasher, and shiny counters everywhere, past a dining room with a fancy-looking glass table and into a living room with the kind of furniture I'd only seen in store windows.

"I'm surprised how new everything looks. How old is the house?" I asked.

Aunt Millie seemed confused, as though this were a tough question, and there was an embarrassing silence.

"Don't let the outside fool you," the sofa said in a high pitched voice. "These places were built to look old—instant age."

A head of short brown hair popped up over the top of the sofa and continued, "Actually this house is only five years old, like most of the ones around here, but since everyone wants a place that looks like an authentic old Cape Cod house, the builder uses preweathered shingles. Do you think that's tacky?"

"Molly, you should be properly introduced before speaking to our guests," Aunt Millie said, shaking her head as though things were never done quite right anymore.

"Hi!" said Molly, leaping over the back of the sofa. "You're Jessie, I remember you from last time you were here, even though I was only a little kid."

"I certainly remember you," said Jessie with a smile. "This is Lou Dunlop. He's a friend of mine from school, and we came out on vacation together."

"Are you staying together? In the same room?" Molly asked, her eyes getting wide.

Jessie laughed and I blushed. Aunt Millie came to the rescue by saying, "No! They are not! And a young lady shouldn't even think, let alone ask, a question like that."

"Sorry," said Molly. With a look of disappointment she flopped into an armchair.

"Where's Uncle Stephen?" Jessie asked.

"He had to run into Boston this morning to see a couple of patients, but he'll be back this afternoon," answered Aunt Millie.

"And David?" I thought Jessie asked a bit too casually.

"He went out for a walk on the beach. He's been acting kind of odd all morning," said Molly with a wink at Jessie.

"Why don't you take your bags upstairs and then see if you can find him?" suggested Aunt Millie, casting a warning look at Molly.

The longer it took to find David, the happier I'd be. But what could I do? The guy lived here.

Aunt Millie showed Jessie to the guest room in the back corner of the house. It wasn't very large, but one wall had a double window that looked out toward the ocean. Then she led me to the front of the house and into a big bedroom. A double bed took up one side of the room and at the foot someone had placed one of those folding roll-away beds.

"I'm afraid we have only one guest room, and I thought it would be easier for you and David to share than to put Jessie in with Molly," Aunt Millie explained apologetically. "I think you'll find that the folding bed is a lot more comfortable than it looks."

"I'm sure it will be fine," I managed to say.

Aunt Millie left me alone to unpack. I threw my underwear down on the folding bed. Not only was I going to have to compete with this guy for Jessie's attention, but I had to sleep at his feet, too. And on a bed that would probably make me into a permanent cripple in a week.

I tried to kick my empty suitcase under the bed, but it jammed and I banged my shin on the heavy metal frame. Swearing quietly, I rubbed my leg and thought I understood now why people usually look so happy when they get back from their vacations.

# Chapter Two

Jessie and I went down the road in front of the house and headed toward the ocean. We were alone, at least for the moment. Aunt Millie had prevented Molly from tagging along by putting her to work cleaning the back porch. But I knew this was only a temporary stay of execution because as soon as we found David our terrific twosome would be a terrible threesome.

The road ended after about fifty yards, and from then on we marched along in sand, the deep soft kind that sucks at your feet and fills your shoes with every step. Jessie was wearing sandals and moving along like a camel, but each of my sneakers felt as if it weighed ten pounds by the time we reached the end.

The end turned out to be a wide path of packed-down sand that ran along the edge of a line of sandy cliffs. I had spent so much time looking down at my feet, that when I raised my head the ocean was suddenly spread out in front of me. We walked to the very edge of the cliff. Way down below was a strip of beach and then there were the waves, rolling in like they had for millions of years, cutting into the sand and making these mountains. In the ocean crashed and out it went, pulling on the beach like it didn't really want to leave.

"Looks like the tide's coming in," said Jessie.

"Washing everything clean," I added.

"You know, the thing I've always liked most about the ocean is that it doesn't change. It's still pretty much the way it was a hundred years ago, or when the Mayflower landed, or even further back than that." She sighed and smiled. "Even if you had a time machine and went back thousands of years, you'd still find the ocean doing exactly what it's doing now. Being here is like standing at the edge of the world and seeing what eternity looks like."

"Everything changes," I said. "Some things are just slower to change than others. This cliff wasn't here a hundred thousand years ago. It's because the change is so gradual that we don't realize it's happening."

Jessie shrugged as though I just wasn't romantic enough to share her dream and walked farther along the cliff.

"Why aren't there any people down on the beach?" I called over to her.

"We're in between two public beaches owned by the town, so unless you live right here, you'd have to park at one of those and walk along the beach for about two miles to get to this spot."

"Do the waves always come in that hard?"

"It's not quite as bad when the tide's going out, but you always have to be a little careful in the water out there."

I scanned the waves and slowly my eyes wandered closer to the base of the cliff as I tried to read the folds in the sand and figure out how far up the water came at high tide. There was something odd at the bottom of the cliff a little off to my left. I walked along the edge until I was exactly above it and squinted down, shielding my eyes from the sun with my hand.

At first I thought it was only a funny mass of seaweed, all black and tangled. But the more I looked, the more the seaweed appeared to be clothes—clothes with a person in them! Somehow it didn't seem like a sunbather. Why wear clothes and huddle in the shadow of the cliffs to sunbathe?

"Jessie, how do you get down to the beach from here?"

"There are some stairs over this way," she answered, motioning to her right, "but let's not go down until we find David."

I was afraid we already had. "There's something down there that I want to check out," I shouted, running toward the stairs.

Even taking them two at a time, it was slow work getting to the beach because the stairs zigzagged down the face of the huge dune, but in a few minutes I was running up the beach to the object I had seen. I stopped short about fifteen feet from whatever it was.

"Hello?" I said nervously, feeling pretty stupid, but I'd feel a lot stupider if it turned out to be someone sleeping on the beach. This way, if anyone answered, I could always comment on the weather and slink away.

But there was no answer. I went closer and moved to the right. I could see his face; it was definitely a guy. He was lying on his side, but the head was bent back at a right angle to his body, so he was staring directly at me. I knew a neck shouldn't bend like that and that eyes should blink. He stared and I stared. It was turning into a contest, but he had a big edge. Slowly I walked closer and carefully lifted his left hand trying not to feel how cold and heavy it was. I couldn't find a pulse, and when I let go it just flopped back into the sand.

"David?" I heard a voice beside me ask. I hadn't noticed Jessie come up. "David!" she said in a more demanding tone, as though he were purposely ignoring her.

Suddenly she rushed toward him. I grabbed her and held tight.

"Look, there's been some kind of accident and David's been hurt. We shouldn't touch him. We have to go back and get help." I hoped she would listen because I didn't have the strength to argue. My body was already shaking so much that I was holding Jessie as much to steady myself as to comfort her.

Finally I put an arm around her shoulders and began to guide her to the stairs. Jessie moved mechanically, not aware of what she was doing. Her eyes stayed wide open just like David's, and before we had reached the stairs she started to moan. It was a low, strangled sound from deep inside of her. I wanted to clamp my hand over her mouth to stop the sound, but I didn't dare. The moaning continued all the way up the stairs, all the way across the sand and all the way to the house.

# *Chapter Three*

I've always wanted to ride in a limousine, but somehow it takes a lot of fun out of it when you're in a funeral procession. But that's where I was, riding along in a big black car with Jessie and Molly, and looking out at the rain. Uncle Stephen, Aunt Millie, and her sister and brother-in-law were in the limousine ahead of us. At the front of the line was the hearse. It was a regular parade. Take it from me, there's nothing worse than a rainy day at the beach, unless it's a rainy day at the beach when you're going to a funeral.

I had offered to go home by bus the day after we found David, but Uncle Stephen asked me to stay to

keep Molly and Jessie company until things sort of
got back to normal. Even though I really didn't want
to be there, I didn't want to leave Jessie behind,
either, so I stayed.

Luckily, Uncle Stephen had been home that afternoon when I got Jessie back from the beach and
stammered out a description of what we had seen.
He listened carefully, asked a few brief questions,
then quickly, but without rushing around and getting everyone upset, he called the police and got an
ambulance sent down to the beach. After that he
asked me, as though I were the one person he could
depend on, to give him a hand getting Jessie upstairs. We carried her up to the guest room, and he
gave her an injection to help her relax. I stayed there
while Uncle Stephen went down to the beach to meet
the ambulance. Gradually Jessie's moaning stopped,
and I left the room when she finally seemed to have
gone to sleep.

Since then, three long days ago, Jessie and Aunt
Millie had both been pretty much out of it. The police had come the next day and questioned me briefly
about what I had seen. They seemed certain that
David had walked too close to the edge and accidentally fallen. Uncle Stephen had convinced them that
Jessie was in no condition to answer questions.
Sometimes you'd get a little smile when you spoke to
her, but it was like she couldn't really hear what you
said because she was too busy listening to some other

voice that only she could hear. I guess the shock of finding your favorite cousin all twisted up on the beach can do that to you.

When Jessie did talk, it was usually to Aunt Millie. They would have these long, rambling conversations about what a great guy David had been. Aunt Millie would recall every little thing he had done from birth until the day he died, and Jessie would get sort of dreamy and say how kind and funny he had been that summer they had spent together. It was like being in a room where everyone spoke a foreign language. Now and then one of them would look at me, and I would smile and nod. But I didn't know or care what he had done at the age of nine; and the one time I had seen him, he hadn't been at his best. I was starting to dislike David more dead than I had alive, and that was saying something. After a while the whole thing got awfully boring, and although I know it's not nice to say, I was kind of glad they were finally going to put him in the ground.

"Did they have to cut him open?" Molly asked, sliding toward me on the large limousine seat. I quickly glanced over to see if Jessie had heard the question, but she continued staring out the window as if there were really something to see out in the rain.

"I don't think so," I whispered. "It was pretty obvious, according to Uncle Stephen, that he had broken his neck in the fall. The medical examiner only needed to do a brief examination."

"That's good. David was always pretty conceited about his body. He wouldn't want it to look bad for the funeral."

I gave Molly a careful look to see if she was joking, but she just sat there appearing innocent and proper in her dark gray dress. Somehow, maybe because she spent most of her time reading while Jessie and Aunt Millie reminisced about what a great guy David had been, I suspected that she might know something about her brother that they didn't.

I always like to know the truth about things, and it was really bothering me that everyone was pretending that David was perfect just because he was dead. How did I know they were wrong? Well, sure, I was jealous, I admit it. But no one could be as wonderful as they were making him out to be. Everyone had some flaws. Somehow Jessie had to see that David had had some, too, or I would never stand a chance with her. You can't compete with the dead, especially when people remember them as being better than they were.

I edged over toward Molly and looked at Jessie again to make sure she wasn't paying attention.

"Was your brother conceited about a lot of things?"

At first I thought Molly wasn't going to answer, but then she started to speak, softly and quickly.

"Yeah, he thought he was pretty great, and in a lot of ways he was. David was good-looking, great at sports and smart about things that mattered to him. People always liked him."

"Sounds like a nice guy," I said, my disappointment showing.

Molly gave me a sidelong glance. "He could be, but he wasn't always. One summer he worked over at Miss Drake's house. She was his high school principal and a stuffy old lady. He mowed the lawn, painted the fence and fixed storm windows. She always paid him, but after a while he was staying and having lemonade or iced tea with her on the back porch. I didn't believe it, so one day he took me along. It was incredible! One of the meanest people in the school, and she was stuffing him with cookies, cake and tea, all the while talking about her nephews and their children. When she wasn't looking, he turned to me and winked. It was all a game to him. I asked him how he did it, and he said, 'Pretend to like people, and they'll do things for you.'"

"What did she do for him aside from feed him?"

"Wrote college recommendations. Once she wrote those..." Molly stopped and shook her head. "Miss Drake called one day in the winter to ask if David could come over and shovel snow. He told me to say he wasn't home. When I asked why, he just smiled and said, 'I don't need the old bag anymore.'''

"Sweet guy."

"But he could be," Molly protested softly. "Sometimes he was the sweetest guy in the world. In fact the morning of the day he died, he said that he had a surprise for me."

"What kind of surprise?"

"He wouldn't tell me, but he said that it was really big and he might give it to me very soon. But all he gave me then was a hint."

I waited, but she didn't go on. "Okay, Molly, what was the hint?"

Satisfied that I was interested, she continued. "He said that it was something that's white and black and red all over."

"That's an easy one."

She frowned. "Okay, smart guy, what could be three colors at the same time?"

"A newspaper," I answered. "It's black and white, and you *read* it all over. That's an old one."

"Yeah, a lot older than I am, I guess. But I wonder why David would surprise me with a newspaper?"

I wonder, too, I thought, as the procession came to a halt in front of the church. Maybe David just had a sense of humor and liked to tease his sister.

Our Lady of the Dunes it said on the church sign. With his sense of humor, David would probably have appreciated that. Then again, maybe not.

## Chapter Four

The funeral went okay until the very end at the cemetery, when people realized that David wasn't going to climb out of the box, say it was all a mistake and go back home with his happy family. Aunt Millie's sister was the first to start crying, but pretty soon Aunt Millie joined in; and although she didn't make any noise, tears were running down Jessie's face, as well.

Even my eyes were a bit wet. Maybe it was contagious or maybe it was seeing Jessie cry, but probably it was because every funeral sort of reminds me of my mother's. That was a rainy day, too, but in October; and the dirt they threw on the coffin was almost mud—somehow that made it worse, being buried in mud.

Other than the family, not many people were there to say goodbye to David. There were a few neighbors from the Cape, two friends of the family from Boston and the guy who owned the shop in Provincetown where David had been working. He was in his early twenties, his skin wasn't very good and he had kind of a thin, slippery look about him that reminded me of a weasel. All through the graveside service, he kept looking at Jessie in a way I didn't care for, but Jessie was in no condition to notice.

As we got back in the cars to leave the cemetery, Uncle Stephen helped Aunt Millie into the limousine and then invited everyone to come back to the house for a while. I saw that the Weasel accepted.

Since I wasn't part of the family, I didn't want to be in the way, so I stayed in a corner of the living room after helping myself to some punch and a sandwich. A party after a funeral always seems to me a little weird, like saying, "Hey, let's celebrate! Death didn't get us this time!" I suppose that's as good a reason for a party as any, but somehow it seems a little selfish, you know. Fifteen minutes after the coffin hits the bottom of the hole, everyone is back talking about their cars, jobs and vacations.

After a while Molly got off the sofa, where she had been sitting with her mother and Jessie, and settled down on a hassock next to me.

"How's it going?" I asked.

She shrugged. "Okay, I guess it just bothers me that everyone is making such a fuss over David, but most of them never really knew him."

"What about your mother?"

"Oh, she's nice, but she never really knows what's going on at home. During the school year she teaches second grade and that takes almost all of her time. Stephen knew David better than Mom ever did."

Calling her stepfather by his first name threw me for a minute. I looked across the room and saw him talking to the friends from Boston. He was listening in that quiet, careful way that I remembered from my own time with a shrink after Mom died. But my shrink had been a bald-headed guy with a bad leg, while Uncle Stephen had a full head of dark curly hair and moved like an athlete.

"Didn't David have any friends?"

"I guess all his college friends are out in California. During the last four years, he only came home at Christmas. He stayed out there and worked in the summers. I don't think he stayed in touch with anyone from high school."

"I'm surprised he didn't stay in California after he graduated."

"So were we. We went out to see him graduate, and he said he'd fly back with us. We were all kind of shocked because he seemed to like California so much, but all he'd say was that there were some great opportunities out here."

"What did he major in?" I asked.

"Business," Molly answered. "He said that before long he'd be in business for himself."

"But right now he was working for that guy?" I asked, nodding in the direction of the Weasel, who was just coming down the stairs from the second floor.

"Terry McCoy. Yeah, he runs The Leather Place in Provincetown," Molly said, wrinkling her nose. "I think he's kind of creepy."

Obviously she was a fine judge of character. Terry saw us looking, and since Jessie wasn't paying any attention to him, he swaggered across the room to us. At least he tried to swagger; it's hard to be impressive when you're a weasel.

"Hi there, little Molly, how are you doing?" he asked.

"Pretty good, little Terry."

His mouth curved up on the sides into a sharklike smile. "I forgot what a smart girl you can be, especially when it comes to your mouth. Who's your pal?" he asked, barely glancing in my direction.

Molly introduced us and I shook his hand. It was like squeezing a wet sponge that's been in the sink overnight—cold and limp.

"So you're Jessie's friend," he said. "You're a lucky guy. She's real cute. The only thing is, she doesn't seem like much fun."

"Could be she's upset over the death of David. You *do* remember your friend David, don't you?" asked Molly.

Terry chuckled and reached out to pat her on the head, but she ducked from under his hand and moved closer to me.

"I won't hurt you," he said with a phony look of surprise. "After all, I was your brother's best friend."

"When did you and David first meet?" I asked.

He gave me a long stare as if it were a trick question, then he answered carefully, "We first met in June at The Leather Place."

"And this is August. I guess you make best friends fast," I said.

"I'm just a friendly guy," he said, bobbing his long bony face as though laughing to himself. "And we had a lot in common."

If David had much in common with this guy, then he certainly wasn't as pure as everyone was saying.

"Stop by the shop sometime and bring Jessie along. She'd look great in a pair of leather pants," Terry said with a leer, and wandered across the room.

"*He* was your brother's best friend?" I asked.

"Yeah, sort of. David was always telling me what a sleazy character he was, but they spent a lot of time together in that shop."

"What's The Leather Place like?"

"It's a little store near the center of Provincetown. They have all these handcrafted leather things. You know, everything from jackets and vests to watchbands. They don't make the stuff themselves. David used to joke that it was made by a lost tribe of Indians on Long Island," said Molly with a faint smile.

"Do they sell much?"

"I never saw anyone in that place the two or three times I was there."

"Why did Terry hire your brother if the shop isn't busy?"

Molly frowned. "I don't know how David got the job. A few days after we came out here this summer, he announced that he was going to work there."

"Somehow Terry doesn't look responsible enough to own a store," I said, watching him slide over next to Aunt Millie.

"I don't know if he owns the place or just manages it, and I think he takes a course or two at the community college out here."

"Hello, you two. Are you doing okay?" a deep, soft voice asked. I looked up and saw Uncle Stephen standing over us.

"We're just fine, Stephen," Molly answered with a smile.

"Would you please go over and help your mother up to the bedroom, Molly? She has a headache and should lie down for a little while."

"Sure," said Molly, uncurling from the hassock.

"I'm glad you two are getting along so well," he said, watching her walk across the room and take Aunt Millie's arm, guiding her away from the Weasel.

"She's a good kid."

He leaned closer to me, and I could smell his after-shave. "I also want to thank you for staying on to help. It's been a difficult time for all of us, of course, but your being here has made things easier."

I was embarrassed because I really hadn't done that much. "That's okay," I mumbled.

"I have to get back to my patients tomorrow, and I was wondering if you would consider staying for another week. It might be good to have someone here who didn't know David and who would be able to get people's minds onto other things. I know you originally planned to visit for two weeks anyway, and although I'm sure things haven't been very pleasant for you, they might improve a bit now that the funeral is over."

He hesitated and looked over at Jessie, who was slumped down on the sofa, staring at the floor. It was hard to believe that anyone so pretty could become so lifeless. Even her hair looked limp.

Stephen continued. "Actually, it's for Jessie's sake as much as anyone else's that I want you to stay. She was apparently very attached to David, even though they hardly knew each other. That one summer she spent with him when she was thirteen and very impressionable led her to form an image of David as the ideal man."

What was I, chopped liver? I wondered.

"Now that David's dead," Uncle Stephen said softly, "she's got a lot of work to do to get her mind in order."

I nodded. "But she won't even talk to me. There isn't much that I can do."

"You have to give her time," he said, looking me in the eye. "You're her link with reality, and the one person who will still be with her when she goes back home. Just be there when she wants to talk and try to encourage her to do things, anything that gets her back in touch with life."

"I'll do what I can," I promised. What else could I say?

"I know you will," he said, briefly putting his hand on my shoulder. "And it doesn't have to be all hard work. Get Molly to show you around the Cape. That should keep you busy," he added as he stood up.

Maybe I could keep busy, I thought, and along the way find out some more about Cousin David. Someday I might need to know the truth about him in order to hang on to Jessie.

# *Chapter Five*

The next morning I crawled out of the folding bed feeling stiffer but happier than I had been for a week. Now that the funeral was over, maybe things would begin to get back to normal—normal as in vacation. If I was really lucky, I might even get to move off the cot and use David's nice, soft double bed.

But over breakfast it sounded more likely that the bed, along with the rest of the room, would be turned into a shrine. Uncle Stephen had left early for Boston. But there were only three of us there: Molly and I and half of Aunt Millie and half of Jessie. They were like sleepwalkers who only awakened when someone mentioned the magic word "David." While

Molly and I studied the cereal in our bowls, the same kind of cereal we'd had every morning since my arrival, Aunt Millie and Jessie made plans for sorting through David's things and straightening up his room. Aunt Millie wanted to put clean curtains on the windows, and Jessie was going to sort through his books and put them in alphabetical order. It was sad to listen to them. Sad, but a little scary, too.

Aunt Millie insisted that Molly help them, so right after breakfast, giving me an apologetic little smile, she marched up the stairs behind her mother, leaving me to shift for myself. Before anyone could suggest that I stay around to help, I bolted out the door and headed for the beach. As I went down the road I was surprised to realize that I was humming to myself. Alone, at least, I didn't have to be officially sad.

When I reached the cliffs, instead of going directly to the stairs that led to the beach, I walked to the edge and looked down. Then gradually, a little embarrassed by my curiosity, I slowly moved along the cliffs until I was at the spot from which David must have fallen. The edge was covered with packed sand and a little higher than the path. He would have had to walk off the path by two or three feet in order to fall over. Maybe he was just standing there enjoying the view when . . .

"Watch it, sonny, you could fall from there."

I turned and suddenly felt dizzy. Maybe it was the surprise. I shifted my weight and took a couple of steps away from the edge. In front of me stood an old woman who could have just finished playing the witch in "Hansel and Gretel." She had a long face with a nose to match; it even had a wart on the top. She was wearing a faded tan dress that reached down almost to her shoes and carrying a bag with BLOOMINGDALE'S written on the side. It looked to be filled with empty cans and bottles.

"Somebody fell off there only a few days ago," she said, squinting up at me.

"I know. I'm staying with his family."

"Ah, then maybe you were the one who was with him?"

"With him when?"

"That day."

"You mean the day when he fell? He was alone then, wasn't he?"

She shifted her bag nervously. The cans and bottles rattled hollowly like an eerie drum.

"It's a strangeness," she muttered.

"Did you see him fall? Was someone there with him?" I asked too quickly.

She took a couple of steps away from me, going farther down the path. "When you get old, you don't see so well. Sometimes you don't see things that are there, sometimes you see things that aren't," she croaked.

"Even if you only think you saw something, you should go to the police," I warned, taking a step toward her.

She clutched the bag close and scurried down the path. When she had gone about twenty feet and was certain I hadn't chased her, she turned around, seemingly lost in thought.

"It's a strangeness, it's a strangeness," she said, shaking her head.

The only thing strange around here is you, I thought as I watched her leave, looking like a pile of old clothes moving along the cliff path. Against the background of sand her tan dress quickly blended in, and at fifty yards she was almost invisible.

I immediately started back to the house. Maybe Molly would know who could have been walking along the cliff with David that afternoon. Why hadn't the person come forward to explain what had happened? The only answer made me shiver even in the warm morning sun.

The house was quiet, too quiet, when I got back. There was no sound from upstairs, and when I went to look, David's room was empty and the doors to both Aunt Millie's and Jessie's rooms were closed. I retreated to the first floor and wandered onto the porch. Molly was sitting in the corner of a chaise lounge reading a book.

"What happened? Why is everything so quiet?"

"We hit a snag right away," Molly said, twisting her mouth. "Mom couldn't find David's scrapbook."

"Scrapbook?"

"Yeah, well it was really a book full of newspaper clippings about him. It told all the great things he had done and really impressed the dim-witted girls." Molly frowned. "I never realized that it meant so much to Mom. When we couldn't find it, Mom began to cry, and pretty soon she and Jessie were both crying—a regular duet. I came down here. After a while I guess they both got tired and went to bed."

"Maybe the book is back at the house in Boston?"

"No, we've both seen it here. David had it out a few weeks back to add a clipping about his graduation, and he always kept it on the same shelf. It's really strange that it's missing."

Yeah, almost a strangeness, I thought.

"Molly, did you ever read a story by Edgar Allen Poe called 'The Purloined Letter'?"

Molly shook her head. "But I read 'The Pit and the Pendulum.' It was good but weird."

"Yeah, well in 'The Purloined Letter' this guy wants to hide a letter he's stolen, so he puts it right out in the open on a table with a bunch of other letters."

"Sure! Nobody would think to look for it there," said Molly excitedly.

"Maybe that's what David did with that surprise for you. If it was from a newspaper, what better place to hide it than with other clippings?"

"So you think that somebody stole the book in order to get David's surprise," said Molly thoughtfully. "But who could have taken it then besides someone who lives here?"

"There were lots of people here yesterday, particularly Terry. We even saw him come down from upstairs. He could have pretended to go up to the bathroom, taken the book and slipped it out under his shirt. If he put it in the back, we'd never have seen it under his sport coat."

"It's possible," said Molly, giving me an admiring look. "You know, you're really pretty smart. Jessie wrote to us last year about how you and she had figured out who killed a girl in your school, but I thought maybe you were just lucky. Now I see it was brains."

"Jessie helped a lot, too."

"She isn't much help now," Molly said simply.

She was right, and it bothered me. Jessie had always been the tougher of the two of us. The one who would rush in, while I still wanted to discuss the plan. Now all she could do was cry and sleep. Maybe she had been in love with the guy, and yet, she had hardly known him. If that was love, it was sick. I was still here for her. Didn't that matter?

"Maybe I could, well, could sort of take Jessie's place, and we could try to find out what happened to my surprise," Molly suggested, looking at the floor. Then she added quickly, "Just until Jessie is better."

Why not? I thought. Uncle Stephen was right. It would be good to see the Cape with someone who knew her way around, and I could do some investigating along with the sight-seeing. And maybe if we found out about Molly's surprise, I would learn some things about David that would show what he was really like.

"Fine," I said. "Let's go to Provincetown and visit The Leather Shop."

"Great!" she shouted, leaping up. "I'll go write a note for Mom."

I smiled as she ran from the room. Even though Molly was still a kid, she reminded me of Jessie, of how she had been, and all of a sudden I felt tired and sad.

## Chapter Six

After Molly wrote the note we rummaged around in the refrigerator and found enough meat and cheese left over from the party to make a couple of sandwiches to take with us for lunch. I threw a couple of bottles of soda in a bag with some ice, and that reminded me of what I had wanted to ask Molly when I first came into the house.

"Did you ever see an old woman in a faded brown dress wandering along the cliffs?"

"Sure, that's the Bottle Woman."

"The Bottle Woman?"

"Yeah, she just showed up one summer a couple of years ago. She moved into an old shack down by the abandoned lighthouse. You always see her around the public beaches pulling empty bottles and cans out of the garbage, but she won't touch beer cans or bottles. I asked her why once, and she said she didn't hold with drinking alcohol."

So at least she hadn't been drunk that afternoon, I thought.

"What does she do with the bottles?" I asked.

"I guess she does what most people do, turns them in at the stores for the refund," Molly said. "She must make enough to live on, such as it is. Why do you want to know? Did you see her?"

"I just met her this morning along the cliffs," I said cautiously.

At first when I had come back from talking to the Bottle Woman, I had been ready to tell Molly everything, but now I wasn't so sure that it was worth stirring things up all over again until I had some solid proof that another person actually had been with David that afternoon.

I decided that Molly would have to wait until I knew more, so before she could ask any questions about the Bottle Woman, I said, "Ready to go?"

Her eyes brightened, and she rushed upstairs. In five minutes she was back down wearing lipstick, some eye shadow, and with her short brown hair brushed until it shone. She was cute but kind of funny. Some twelve-year-old girls can get away with pretending to be sixteen or so, but with her skinny, kid's body, Molly looked more like a little girl using her mother's makeup. I was hoping that I hadn't made a mistake in offering to take her along.

We got in Jessie's car and headed toward the main highway. Once we were able to get up some speed, I felt better. It was good to be going someplace, to be moving fast, even if I wasn't sure what I was going to do when I got there.

In about twenty minutes we were in Provincetown, but we had to ride along Commercial Street through the center of town for another twenty before I managed to squeeze the Volkswagen into half a space in a public lot along the wharf. We walked back to Commercial and headed up to where Molly thought The Leather Place was.

You could certainly tell the day visitors from the people who lived there. The long-term residents were artsy types wearing sandals, faded jeans and a variety of washed-out T-shirts advertising local shops. The visitors wore shorts, cameras and frantic expressions as they tried to look in the stores and at the same time dodge the traffic on the narrow street.

Molly looked at two guys standing together in front of a shop window.

"Homosexuals," she informed me matter-of-factly. "There are a lot of them here."

"Oh," I said.

"Do you think you're a homosexual?"

I gave her a stare. I hoped it was a masculine one.

"I didn't think so," she said happily. "Although Stephen says that everyone is, at least a little bit. He says there's nothing wrong with that."

I nodded. Who was I to question a shrink?

"Here's the street," said Molly. It was too big a word for the little alley we turned down. Even if you were looking for it, it would be hard to find. A few doors down we came to a window with The Leather Place stenciled on it in brown.

I walked in all ready to see Terry's sneering face. Instead, there was some rustling behind the counter when the tiny bell over the door rang, and a pretty dark-haired girl popped up from behind the counter lifting a large box. She was a little red in the face from the effort and breathing through her mouth.

For a second she reminded me of Susan McGuire. When I was in eighth grade, Susan always hung around me for help in math. I thought I turned her on because she was always breathing through her mouth like she was really excited. Then she was out of school for a couple of weeks, and when she came back, the heavy breathing stopped—she'd had her adenoids taken out. And so another great romance bites the dust.

"Hi. What can I do for you?" my heavy-breathing beauty asked, setting the box on the countertop with a thump. She was a little older than me, wearing the standard jeans and T-shirt with a leather vest over it.

"We're looking for Terry," I said.

"He's not here right now. Is there something I can help you with?"

I hesitated for a second. "I guess not. This is David Marshal's sister, Molly, and I'm Lou Dunlop, a friend of the family."

"I'm Sandra Felden," she said, reaching out to shake my hand. "I just started here this week. I never met your brother," she said to Molly, "but I was sorry to hear about his accident."

Molly gave her a suspicious look. "David never told me that they were planning to hire someone new."

Sandra looked embarrassed. "I'm only part-time. Terry hired me yesterday. I guess I'm kind of a . . . a replacement for your brother."

I liked the way she looked and her being so polite to Molly, but I couldn't figure out why a nice girl would be working around the Weasel.

"It doesn't seem very busy around here," I said, trying to sound casual. "I'm surprised Terry needs another person."

She smiled. I was really getting her ruffled with my sharp questions.

"The rent is low, and we have some good days. Plus Terry has to go out frequently to buy merchandise, so someone had to mind the store."

"That sounds like a lot of—leather," Molly said with a phony look of innocence as she swatted at a row of belts.

"Terry isn't the owner, is he?" I asked.

"I don't know. Maybe you should come back and ask him," Sandra said, moving us toward the door. Obviously she'd had enough questions.

"Thanks for your help," I said, and herded Molly ahead of me out onto the street. Just as the door was about to close, I stuck my head back inside on impulse.

"One more thing."

"Yes?" she asked politely.

"Tell Terry when you see him that I know someone was with David on the cliffs the afternoon he fell."

She looked as though she were about to say something, then stopped.

"Just tell him that," I concluded, giving her a big smile and a wave as I backed out the door.

As soon as we were on the street, Molly's little fingers grabbed my arm, and she pulled me off into the entryway of a store. It was a toy store, and a large stuffed rabbit stared out through the display window at me with its beady eyes. Her fingers dug into my muscle. I didn't think she had that kind of strength.

"What's this crap about someone being with David on the cliffs that day," she hissed.

"Young ladies shouldn't listen in on other people's conversations."

"Bull!"

"And they shouldn't use language like that."

"I thought we were friends, but if you're going to keep stuff like that secret..." she said, letting go of my arm and stepping away. Tears had started in the corners of her eyes, and when I tried to touch her shoulder, she moved farther away from me.

"Okay," I said. "I'm sorry. I just wanted to find out more before I said anything. It might be nothing at all. I told Sandra because I thought maybe we'd get some reaction from Terry when he found out."

I told her everything about my conversation with the Bottle Woman. Molly's tears slowly disappeared. She was still angry but went on listening until I was done.

"The old lady is strange," she said finally, "but if she's right, it helps explain how he went over the edge. It doesn't have to be an accident. It could have been..." she began, and stopped.

"That's right, he could have been pushed; that would make it murder."

To give her credit, Molly didn't even blink at the idea. All she said was, "Why would anyone do that?"

I shook my head. "I don't know, but I think it must have something to do with that creep Terry and with that book of clippings. That's what I'm trying to find out, but I don't want to upset everyone until I know for sure."

"Okay," she said. "I won't tell anyone, either, and I'll help you."

I must have looked less than thrilled at the offer because right away she went on, "That's what you agreed when I said I'd take Jessie's place. We were going to work together. I may be just a kid, but I know lots of things that I haven't even thought about yet."

I grinned and offered my hand. "Partners?"

She took my hand. "But remember, no more secrets."

"No more secrets," I promised. She checked to see if my fingers were crossed. Fortunately, she couldn't see my toes.

# Chapter Seven

We stopped at an empty stretch of beach just outside Provincetown and had our lunch. Soon there were several sea gulls walking around us, staying carefully outside the range of our arms. Molly threw one a piece of crust. It picked the bread up in its beak and flew off to a dune several yards away and began to eat with quick, jerky pecks.

"Well, this trip certainly turned out to be a waste of time," I said, watching another gull struggle with a slice of bologna I had thrown to it. "Terry wasn't even in the shop, so we didn't find out any more about the clipping book."

"We can always go to see Terry some other time. You should relax and enjoy the day," said Molly, closing her eyes and putting her face up to the sun. "Remember, you're here for a vacation."

"Yeah, I guess with everything that's happened I'd kind of forgotten that."

"Are you planning to go to college after next year?" Molly asked, suddenly changing the subject.

"Sure, I guess so."

"Do you think you'll be going somewhere near Boston?"

"I don't know, I suppose it depends on where I can get in. Why?"

"Oh, I was only wondering if you would be able to visit us sometime."

"I guess I could if I went to college near Boston, but I don't know where I'm going." This whole conversation was making me uncomfortable.

"It would be nice if you could visit."

I nodded.

"You're lucky. Pretty soon you won't have adults telling you what to do. I can't wait until I get older and can be on my own."

"Your folks don't seem so bad."

"They aren't. It's the whole idea of being a kid. I hate it. You know what I mean?"

I shrugged.

"You know, I'm twelve and you're seventeen," she went on. "That's only a difference of five years.

If I were twenty and you were twenty-five, it wouldn't be important at all. Five years doesn't make you an adult and me a child."

"It does when you're only twelve."

"Ha!" said Molly, loudly enough to frighten the sea gulls into flight.

When we got back, Uncle Stephen was home, and he suggested that everyone go down to the beach for a swim. Aunt Millie and Jessie said they were too busy going over David's things, and Aunt Millie went through the whole story of the missing scrapbook again. Uncle Stephen offered to search the room himself that evening, and finally, the two women slowly climbed the stairs to return to their sorting.

That left three of us in the living room giving each other looks of sadness mixed with frustration. Molly said she would rather read than swim.

"You aren't going to let me down, are you?" Uncle Stephen asked me.

"No way. I'll go get into my suit," I replied quickly.

The hike down to the beach left us both sweating in the hot afternoon sun, and the first touch of the water as I cautiously waded out turned my foot numb. But Uncle Stephen just strolled in as though it were as warm as bathwater. When it was about up to his waist, he gave a little leap and dived into a wave.

"It's the easiest way to become accustomed to the cold," he called out to me as he surfaced. "Once you get in, it feels warm."

Quickly, holding my breath, I walked out a few yards more and jumped into a large green wave as it came rolling toward me. For one blinding moment I felt cold all over, even my lungs stopped taking in air; then my body adjusted and, believe it or not, the water did begin to feel warm.

I paddled in place for a moment and looked for Uncle Stephen. I finally spotted him, already well out from shore, methodically swimming toward the horizon. By the movements of his elbows, I could see that he had the strong, unhurried stroke of a good swimmer. I knew I didn't stand a chance of catching him, so I swam out a few more yards, alternating between the breaststroke and a crawl, then I went along parallel to the shore.

It was hard to believe that I had already been at the Cape six days and this was the first time I'd been in the water. But my body knew, and after a few minutes it was begging for a rest, so I flipped over and began floating on my back. Since I had been moving parallel to the shore, I was now almost at the point where David had been found. I lifted my head out of the water, did a gentle backstroke and looked to my right to see how the cliffs appeared from the water.

It was difficult to find the place he had fallen from. I knew it was to the right of the stairs and that the cliff gave a little jut upward right where he must have been standing. Finally I saw it or rather—it saw me! A figure in black was standing at exactly the spot, and its two glass eyes were staring down at me. Binoculars catching the late-afternoon sun.

For a crazy moment I considered swimming into shore as fast as I could, dashing up the stairs two at a time and tackling the spy before he or she could escape. But I knew that before I got halfway there, the person could be miles down the road. Instead I decided to embarrass whoever it was, so I lifted my right arm and gave an unmistakable wave in the direction of the reflection.

At first I thought the figure in black hadn't seen me, and I was about to attempt another wave without drowning when the glint of the binoculars disappeared. The dark figure just stood there for a moment. I couldn't tell from that distance, but somehow I knew that its eyes were staring at me. After a moment the figure disappeared.

Suddenly the water felt cold again. With uneven strokes I swam until my feet touched bottom and then walked the rest of the way in. Even the warm sun on my back didn't stop me from shivering as I rubbed myself as hard as I could with the towel. Finally I just sat on the beach trying to relax.

"Are you okay? You look a little pale," Uncle Stephen said a few minutes later as he came out of the water.

"Yeah, I just hit a cold spot and decided to come in before I got a cramp."

I wanted to talk to someone about what I had seen, but I didn't want to lose control of my investigation. Once I mentioned the figure in black, I figured Uncle Stephen would eventually get everything else out of me about the Bottle Woman and Terry. He was so practical and efficient that he would take over, and it would be out of my hands. So I kept my mouth shut or as shut as I could with my teeth chattering.

"It's not a good thing to overdo on the first day out," Uncle Stephen said warningly. "You should break in gradually and give your body a chance to get acclimated."

I watched him as he dried off. He had quite a body for a middle-aged guy, with a narrow waist and strong shoulders like the kids on the swim team.

"You're a pretty good swimmer," I commented.

"Not as good as I used to be," he said, sitting down beside me. "But it's still my favorite form of exercise."

"Did you swim a lot when you were a kid?"

Uncle Stephen hesitated and squinted out at the waves. "I grew up along the California coast, so we went to the beach a lot."

"One of the Beach Boys?"

"Sort of," he said grinning, "but that seems like a long time ago."

He sighed and leaned back on his elbows. "I read somewhere once that the poet Swinburne would swim so far out to sea that fishermen would catch him in their nets. Can you imagine that? Swimming all alone, out of sight of land, just you and the ocean. When you listen to human problems all the time, it's good to get away to something basic and restful once in a while."

"That's something like what Jessie thinks."

He frowned and leaned on his side facing me. "Neither one of us is doing very well in snapping her out of this depression. She and Millie are just feeding off of each other to keep the morbid atmosphere alive. I didn't realize how serious it was until this business with the scrapbook. Although I hate to say it, especially right after asking you to stay, but maybe it would be best if Jessie were back in her home environment."

"You want us to leave?"

Great, I thought selfishly, one dip in the ocean and it's back home again. And I've spent my wonderful vacation trying to look sad while hearing what a great guy my girlfriend's one true love was.

"I know it's a bad deal for you," said Uncle Stephen, as though he could read my mind. He probably could; after all he was a shrink. "But we have to think of Jessie and Millie."

"When do you want us to leave?"

"How about the day after tomorrow? That way maybe you'll be able to get in some time at the beach tomorrow, and Aunt Millie and Jessie will have a chance to get used to the idea of parting. Actually I think we'll close up the house at the end of the week anyway. School will be starting soon for Molly, and Millie has more friends in Boston."

As we walked to the house, Uncle Stephen talked about some of the clinic work he did, particularly with college kids. I half listened but couldn't keep my mind from wandering back to David's death. Only one full day left and so much to find out.

Uncle Stephen must have thought I was sulking about having to leave because when we reached the house, he put his hand on my shoulder. "Look, try getting Jessie to go out with you somewhere tonight and take her mind off things. Maybe she'll snap out of it. I'll work on Millie at the same time. If there's some sign of improvement, then they'll be no reason for you to leave. Okay?"

I smiled and nodded.

"And remember, Lou, I really do appreciate your help."

It felt good to be taken seriously by someone like Uncle Stephen. And that looked as if it might be the only good thing to come out of this vacation, I thought, as the image of the figure on the cliff returned to my mind and made me shiver.

# *Chapter Eight*

Since I had promised to tell her everything, I took Molly out on the porch before supper and let her know about the dark figure on the cliff. I also explained about having to leave in two days. The first piece of news got her excited because she thought we must be on to something if anyone would bother to spy on me. The second item got her angry, and it was all I could do to convince her not to go to Uncle Stephen and make a scene.

When I asked about a place to go with Jessie that might help pull her out of her depression, Molly gave me a suspicious glance and wanted to know if I was looking for somewhere romantic. I admitted that this might be a good idea, and she grudgingly said that the public beach three miles up the road got a crowd of kids who hung around to watch the moon rise and sometimes stayed to see the sun come up. I thanked her, and she just grunted.

After supper while everyone was still around the table, I asked Jessie if she would like to go out for a while. I could tell she was about to refuse. Aunt Millie had already launched into a description of all that was left to do in David's room, when Uncle Stephen intervened, suggesting that a little jaunt might be good for Jessie while he helped Millie take another look for the scrapbook. Aunt Millie, thrilled at the prospect of a renewed search with fresh reinforcements, stopped objecting to our trip. Jessie shrugged and, without waiting for me, went out to the car.

As we drove up the road to the parking lot for the public beach, I asked Jessie how she felt. She continued staring straight ahead as though I hadn't spoken. Not accepting that, I tried again.

"How do you expect me to feel?" she answered.

I gave up.

When we had parked I grabbed out of the trunk an old army blanket that doubled as a beach blanket and we walked down to the sand. A sign listing about a hundred things that weren't allowed stood at the end of the parking lot. One rule was that no one was allowed on the beach after 9:00 p.m. Somebody had scratched out the "p.m." and substituted "a.m." in spray paint. I pointed it out to Jessie with a smile, but she kept walking.

It was early and the sun was only starting to touch the horizon. Families with children were still on the beach. A kid was trying to get a plastic kite that looked like a deformed bat to fly, and two others were tossing around a Frisbee covered with orange tape that glows in the dark. But scattered along the beach at discreet distances from each other were blankets with teenage couples lying or sitting on them. All believers in the old principle, "Make out while the moon shines."

We had gone only about fifty feet along the beach when Jessie said she was tired and couldn't go on any farther. I looked around to make sure we had enough privacy and spread out the blanket.

As we sat looking out to sea, the world put on a display for us. The sun went a deep red, turning the waves into rolling fire, until the darkness came down like a black curtain to extinguish them. You couldn't see the waves anymore, but you could hear them pound a steady rhythm on the shore. All this happened, and Jessie didn't look up once. She seemed intent on picking at the sleeve of her sweatshirt. There was nothing stuck on it or unraveled, but her fingers busily worked at it as though her life depended on it.

I figured I'd start with the only topic that was sure to bring a reaction.

"Did David like to sit on the beach?"

She nodded.

"Were you ever at this beach with him?"

She sighed and said slowly, "I don't want to talk with you about David."

"Why not?"

"Because you didn't know him."

"I'd like to try."

She shrugged as though what I wanted was a matter of complete indifference to her and returned to pulling at her sleeve.

"Is there any place at the Cape that you'd like to see while we're here?"

She ignored me, so I reached over and gently took the hand that was attacking the sleeve and held it in my own. She let me do it, but her hand lay limply in mine like a dead fish. I released the hand, stroked her hair and tried to look into those light blue eyes I knew so well. Those eyes that I had seen laugh, and joke, and be tender.

She shook her head in annoyance and turned away.

"What's the matter?" I asked.

"David's dead and all you can think about is getting your hands on me."

"That's not fair, Jessie. I've never treated you that way, and I won't now. All I want to do is understand."

"Understand," she said slowly, going back to picking at her sleeve. "What's there to understand? He's dead and nothing will ever be the same."

The sun had been replaced by a full moon that sent a path of white light across the water. It looked as if you could walk right up to it to the moon itself. Right up to the big time where all questions have answers and the streets are paved with chocolate bars. But nobody could make that walk, not without drowning first.

When we got back to the house, Aunt Millie threw her arms around Jessie shouting, "We found it! We found it!"

"Found what?" I asked.

"The scrapbook," answered Molly, watching in amazement as Jessie and Aunt Millie danced around the room. Aunt Millie was doing most of the moving and sort of dragging Jessie along. "I guess we were wrong about its being stolen."

Uncle Stephen came in from the kitchen and stood beside me watching them. From his expression I couldn't tell what he thought about the spectacle.

"I don't know how they overlooked it," he said finally. "Almost as soon as we started to search, I found the scrapbook in the middle of a pile of David's clothes that someone had packed away in a box.

Millie probably put it there right after the funeral and just forgot where it was.''

Jessie and Aunt Millie collapsed on the sofa and were eagerly starting to turn the book's pages. It was about the size of a yearbook, with sheets of heavy construction paper fastened inside a black cover. Each page had one or two newspaper articles pasted on it with a date written at the top.

"How did things go at the beach?" asked Uncle Stephen. Molly glanced up with interest.

I shook my head. "Not very well. She won't even talk about David or anything else for that matter. I think it's going to be a long time before she gets over this."

"Yes, well it's probably for the best that she'll be going home soon. Will her parents be back by the day after tomorrow?"

"I think they'll be home tomorrow."

"Good. I'll give them a call and explain the situation here. Tomorrow morning before I leave for work I'll break the news to Jessie and Millie. There's no sense in telling them now and spoiling their fun," he said sadly, watching them pore over the book as Aunt Millie explained that David had been a star Little League pitcher. He walked over behind the sofa and looked down on them.

"It's great to have a good book to read," Molly whispered.

"But is it fact or fiction?" I whispered back.

"Who knows?" she answered. "Sometimes a scrapbook can be a crapbook."

I felt as if I had been asleep half the night when I heard it: a scratching sound under my window. The illuminated digits on my travel clock greenly glowed 1:15 as I tried to remember if they owned a cat that I had somehow overlooked. I slipped out of bed and moved carefully across to the window and peered through the curtains.

If that was the family cat under my window by the side door, it cast a bigger shadow than any cat I ever wanted to meet. Then the clouds pulled away from in front of the moon, and I saw someone dressed in black kneeling by the side door. By the sound of it, he was trying to open the lock.

What to do? My first impulse was to call Uncle Stephen and let him decide. But in the back of my mind I suspected that this noisy sneak thief had to have something to do with David's death. In fact, it was probably Terry, back for a second shot at the scrapbook.

Quickly and quietly—I hoped—I moved down the hall and stairs to the first floor. For a moment I considered going through the kitchen to the side door, suddenly whipping it open and inviting the startled intruder in for coffee and a chat. But I wasn't sure how the locks on the side door worked. By the time I got it opened, he could have a hundred-yard head start down the road or a gun pointed at my chest.

So instead I moved to the front door, tripped over a chair that tried to jump me and, sounding not quite as loud as a cavalry charge, reached my destination. The thought of a gun leveled at my chest had got me thinking about a weapon, so I grabbed Molly's tennis racket off the hall table as I went by. It might not be much, but some of my opponents have suggested that in my hands it's a deadly weapon, especially when I accidentally send it sailing over the net. After fumbling with the key and bolt for several seconds I got the front door opened and edged my way out onto the front porch.

How was I to know that a flowerpot would be on the top step? Down it went with a crash, bouncing off each step. I stood still for a moment, shocked by what I had done, then I realized that there was no time to lose. Forgetting about silence, I raced around the house to the side door ready to attack him with my powerful first serve. There was nothing but darkness. I squinted, but there was no one by the side door. I saw how the trees cast bands of shadow over the house and the way the hose lay coiled at the side of the driveway like a snake waiting to strike. I saw Uncle Stephen's car parked in the driveway like a giant beast sleeping after a long journey. I saw all those things that look normal and cheery in the daylight and strange and scary in the night; but I didn't see a single figure in black.

I went up the drive to the side door. Even in the bright moonlight I couldn't make out if anything had been done to the lock. I tried the door but it didn't open. With Uncle Stephen's car parked behind me, I crept around the side of the house, the tennis racket firmly in my hand. Could we be chasing each other around the house? I had a funny image of the two of us circling until dawn, the one never catching the other. Keeping my left hand on the wall to guide me, I slowly went along, constantly looking to my right in case the intruder was lying in the sand waiting to jump me.

I was about five feet from where the garbage cans stood in a small cart when something gave me a powerful shove in the small of my back that sent me flying. My neck snapped back, then forward. The racket flew out of my hand, sailing off somewhere into the yard, and I went into the garbage.

For a second I was stunned. Had anyone gotten the number of that car? Car, heck, it was more like a steamroller. Slowly I raised my face out of what smelled and felt like chicken bones mixed with cold succotash, staggered to my feet and looked behind me. Of course, there was nothing but darkness. Up the road in the distance I heard a car engine start up.

Only a weasel like Terry would have hidden behind Uncle Stephen's car, waited until I went by, then attacked me when my back was turned. It was a cowardly act. I wished I had done it to him instead.

I walked to the front of the house, went inside, locked the door, and made my way into the downstairs bathroom. Fortunately the garbage cans had been made of plastic, so no one had been awakened by my swim in suet. Of course, a broken flowerpot hadn't gotten much of a reaction, either. Heavy sleepers lived in this house. I scrubbed my face and hair under the sink faucet using deodorant soap until they smelled squeaky clean. Then quietly I went back upstairs to bed.

Even if I hadn't caught him, at least I could tell Molly I had scared away a potential thief, I thought as I tried to put myself to sleep by counting heads that looked like Terry's being hit over a tennis net.

# Chapter Nine

When I came downstairs the next morning, Molly was on the sofa with her feet tucked under her and David's scrapbook propped up on her knees.

"I see you finally got up, sleepyhead," she remarked.

"Anything interesting among the scraps?" I asked, sitting down awkwardly next to her. My back and neck were both stiff and weren't quite bending right.

"A lot of the early stuff I never knew about, but there's nothing that comes as a big surprise."

"Is there anything that doesn't seem to belong, especially among the recent clippings?"

Molly flopped half the book over on my lap, and starting about five pages from the end we went through each page until there was nothing but blank pages. There were articles on David's graduation, on his participation in a road race, on his election to a business fraternity and a small piece on an internship he had served in a chemical company. It was all very predictable and of no help at all.

Molly sighed and began to close the book.

"Let's look at the blank pages in the back," I said.

"Okay, but there's nothing on them. I already looked."

Starting with the last page that had an article on it, she leafed through the five or six pages remaining in the book.

"Hold it!" I said as we reached the next to the last page.

"Why?" asked Molly. "It's just another empty page."

"Look at these," I said, pointing to four spots that looked a little bit lighter than the rest of the page. "Something's been removed from here."

Molly examined the spots closely. "Something has been removed all right, but David might have taken it out himself."

"Sure, but let's just speculate. Maybe the book was stolen like we thought originally, but suppose whoever took it brought it back. Before they did, though, they removed the article that David was going to surprise you with."

"That's a lot of supposing?"

"Yeah, but strange things have been happening around here," I said, and explained about my bout with the mysterious stranger.

"Wow! You should have gotten me up to give you some help." She squinted into the distance and seemed lost in thought. "But why would he be trying to break in if he had already stolen and returned the scrapbook?"

"You've got me. Maybe it wasn't the same person. There seems to be plenty of crime to go around on this one."

I got up and went toward the kitchen. Molly whispered, "Before Stephen went to work he told them that you and Jessie were leaving tomorrow."

If they were upset, I couldn't tell. The two of them just sat there doing their zombie imitations. When I asked Jessie if she wanted to go for a swim this afternoon, she looked at me for several seconds, then shook her head.

"Why not?" I asked calmly. I was determined not to sound annoyed.

She looked up from her bowl of the usual soggy cereal. "I feel tired," she said, and got to her feet and shuffled out of the kitchen. I heard her going up the stairs with less speed than some eighty-year-olds.

"What's wrong with her?" Molly asked in exasperation.

"She's upset about David," said Aunt Millie, staring at us as though somehow we weren't filling the bill.

Molly was about to say more, but I shook my head. Aunt Millie wasn't in any better shape than Jessie.

"We'll never get his room fixed up right," Aunt Millie continued, leaning back in the chair and letting her arms fall helplessly at her sides. "It's the last straw!" Her face got red and she began to cry.

Molly ran over and hugged her. I stammered something about meeting her down on the beach in a few minutes and went outside. I picked up the remains of the geranium I'd knocked over and tried to plant it in the sand near the foot of the porch. I hid the pieces of the pot under the garbage I had come to know so intimately the night before. Molly's racket was sitting on a mound of sand about twenty feet in back of the house. I put it on the side steps where someone would be sure to notice it.

The sun was shining so brightly that it was difficult to imagine how sinister everything had seemed the night before. But it had happened. The night was as real as the day, and the hidden truth about David was starting to appear more real than what most people wanted to believe.

I took off my sneakers and walked along in the sand, which was already warm and would be too hot to walk on by afternoon. When I got down to the beach, I stood watching the waves come banging into shore. Maybe Jessie had been right, and nothing ever really did change in the ocean. People couldn't plow it, build on it or cover it with cement like they could with fields and meadows; and they couldn't cut holes through it or run roads over it the way they did with mountains. It just was. Rolling in and rolling out on its own mysterious schedule. There was something monotonous but at the same time restful about it. Restful like that last moment before going to sleep, when you just let go and nothing really seems to matter. I could see how that poet Uncle Stephen had told me about could want to keep on swimming and swimming toward a horizon that was always just out of reach.

"Lou," Molly called from a few yards behind me. I barely heard her over the surf.

"How's your mother?" I asked as we started along the beach.

"Mom decided that she was tired, too, and went upstairs to lie down. I asked if she wanted me to stay, but she didn't seem to care."

Molly picked up a few stones worn smooth by the ocean and threw them ahead of us down the beach.

"You know, I keep wondering..." she began. "I know this is going to sound selfish, but I keep won-

dering if Mom would be this upset if I had died instead of David. She's hardly seen him in four years,
but I really think she feels worse about losing him
than she would if I had died. Is that a terrible thing
to think?''

"It's natural. I don't have any, but aren't brothers
and sisters always competing for things?''

"Yeah, but this doesn't seem right somehow, you
know. It's like I didn't want her to be sorry that David is gone.'' With a sideways tilt of her head she
gave me a worried look. I felt sorry for her.

"If it makes you feel any better, I've been wondering the same thing about Jessie. Would she be
upset if I had been the one at the bottom of the cliff?
I'm jealous of David even though he's dead.''

"Well, don't be!'' said Molly with anger in her
voice. "He was my brother and I loved him, but
Jessie would have been crazy to like him better than
you. He never really cared much about anyone other
than himself. That's why, even though girls liked him
because of his looks, they never stayed around for
long. But you, well, you're special,'' she said blush-
ing, and staring furiously at the sand.

Determined to keep the conversation off Molly
and me, I asked, "Did David go out with anyone
special this summer? I was surprised that there were
no girls at the funeral.''

"Early in the summer he went out with Carolyn
Hayes. Her folks have a big place on the Bay. But it

didn't last much more than a month. I think even David was kind of sorry when they broke up."

"Do you think he could have been meeting a girl on the cliffs that day?"

"Could be," Molly said, and pointed up to the top of the cliff where a white lighthouse trimmed in red stood. "Somebody used to live there, but now they're all automated. I guess some kind of computer turns them off and on. The house where the Bottle Woman lives is in the woods behind it."

We went up a long gradual slope of packed sand that led from the beach to the lighthouse. Sure enough, about a hundred yards behind it was a house in the woods. You could call them woods if you used the word loosely; they were more like waist-high weeds with a few struggling pine trees mixed in; and you could call it a house, if a building with four sides and a roof is all it takes to make a house. Even at that, half the shingles were off the roof, making it look like a jigsaw puzzle someone had forgotten to finish, and the sides were peeling paint as though it had a sunburn.

"Does she live out here by herself?" I asked as we followed the winding path through the weeds.

"Her son lives with her," said Molly, pounding on the door, "but he's only a little kid."

No one answered, so I banged on it a few times. There wasn't a sound, but the door slowly swung open a few inches. Without hesitation Molly pushed it open and went inside. I wasn't sure this was a good idea, but I couldn't let her go alone.

It was like being blinded and suffocated at the same time. Only a few thin shafts of light filtered through the heavy curtain on the one small window, and the smell was that disgustingly sweet kind that honeysuckle gives off late in the season.

Molly walked over to the window and pulled back the curtains. Both of us squinted as sunlight poured into the room, raising the temperature from 100 to 110. The whole shack was one room. On the right was a small kerosene stove with a pyramid of canned food piled up next to it. To the left was a door leading to a small closet with a toilet and sink.

The entire center of the room was taken up by two large wooden bins: one filled almost to the top with empty soda bottles and the other half-filled with soda cans. A swarm of flies, disturbed by the sunlight, circled frantically above the bins. A few of the braver ones cautiously returned to their perches. Nothing was going to spoil their dinner.

"There's nothing like the garbage dump on a hot day," I said, walking around to the other side of the bins. "You can see all sorts of natural processes at work."

"Like rot, mold and decay," Molly said, wrinkling up her nose.

Behind the bins a mountain of dirty blankets was piled on the floor. I gave it an idle kick. Suddenly it moved!

"Ma?" the mountain said.

I wanted to say, "Yeah, go back to sleep, honey," but my tongue kept flopping in my mouth like a beached whale.

The blankets fell away as the mountain stood up and stood up, until it towered over me. The blankets slipped to the side, and way up there I could make out a face, kind of flat and with short hair on top. The body was huge but had the soft look of molded Jell-O. But even a ton of Jell-O can crush you.

"You're not Ma," he said, peering down at me.

Maybe I could be—just for the day, I thought.

He stepped forward and his body pushed me back against one of the bins. I tried to shove him away, but my hands just sank into his flesh, never reaching muscle or bone. It was like fighting mashed potatoes. That was the ridiculous thought I had, as the bin dug into my spine and my lungs struggled to suck in air.

"Stop that!" I heard a voice in the distance shout. "That's not nice!"

I could dimly see Molly standing next to him, looking up and shouting. He stared down at her the way an elephant might watch an ant before stepping on it. I wanted to tell Molly to get out of there, to run, but I couldn't get enough breath. The room started to go black and white, then it slowly began to revolve around in circles. Instead of being scared, I felt as if I was far away watching something happen to me.

"You stop or I'll tell your Ma!" Molly shouted.

Slowly the pressure stopped. I leaned gasping on the side of the bin as my lungs pulled in air. Gradually the world began to look right again—not rosy, but okay.

"Where is your ma?" Molly demanded of the giant, who stood there with his arms dangling at his sides.

"Out," he grunted.

"When will she be back?" Molly continued.

His shrug set off a tidal wave of flesh that rippled across his body.

"I was sleeping," he said, giving me an accusing glance. Here we go again, I thought.

"Sorry we bothered you. Why don't you go back to sleep," I suggested with my friendliest smile, while pushing Molly ahead of me toward the door.

The giant stood rooted to the spot, but his small eyes followed us as we crossed the room and went out the door. As soon as we hit the path, without saying anything, we walked faster and faster until we were down on the beach again.

I stopped and turned to Molly. "I thought you said he was a little kid?"

She grinned guiltily. "I meant mentally."

"Great! That's swell! You almost got me killed for a joke. Two people have tried to break me in half within the last twelve hours. It's starting to get me down."

"Well I didn't tell you to kick him. And who saved your miserable life?"

I ignored that. "I thought we were going to tell each other the truth—no more secrets. Or did you forget that already?"

She looked sheepish, but there was a gleam in her eye. "I owed you one for not telling me about the Bottle Woman in the first place."

"That's a pretty childish attitude."

"I am a child!" she blurted out, and instantly seemed to regret it.

She had me there, but before I could come back with a really crushing answer, two flashes of light reflected off the cliff above us.

Without a word I ran back up the slope to the lighthouse, but before I had gotten halfway up a figure in black stood up and started running. I tried to put on some speed, but my feet kept slipping in the loose sand. By the time I reached the top, all I could see was the back of a red car speeding down the road.

"Who was it?" asked Molly when she reached my side.

"Somebody who wants to know what we're up to."

Molly stared forlornly down the road. "I wish we had an answer to that one ourselves," she said softly.

## Chapter Ten

After lunch I went up to my room, or rather David's room, to lie down for a while. It was the first afternoon that Jessie and Aunt Millie hadn't been in there packing things. Even so, you would hardly know that anything was gone. A couple of cardboard boxes in the corner were filled with clothes, but all the books and records still seemed to be on the shelves. I guess it slows down packing when you tell a story about each piece.

I tossed around on the stupid folding bed for a while, decided I couldn't sleep and browsed through the stuff on the shelves. All I saw were a lot of books on business, sports and travel. There wasn't even a good mystery for me to spend the afternoon reading.

Of course, I had more than enough mystery right around me: missing books, dark strangers and fatal walks on cliffs. What I didn't have was much time. We were scheduled to leave tomorrow after lunch. When I had reminded Jessie earlier in the afternoon that we were leaving tomorrow, she seemed to take it with the same indifference as everything else, although I saw a little flicker of fear in her eyes. Maybe Uncle Stephen was right, and she had gotten too comfortable staying here with her grief.

I looked out the window. The sky was that clear dark blue that looked like a painting and made you imagine that with a telescope you could see around the world. Such a big ocean. You had to admire those guys who would sail around the world in small wooden ships hunting for whales. They didn't give up, and as long as there was some time left, neither would I. Terry was at the center of this somehow. It was just too much of a coincidence that right after I told him that I knew someone had been with David when he died that the dark figure with binoculars turned up.

I found Aunt Millie in the living room dozing over some knitting, and told her that I had to run into Provincetown to do some shopping. Even when I said that I'd have supper out she hardly looked up. Molly was out on the porch reading a book. I was tempted to slip out without telling her, especially after the trick she had pulled on me with King Kong. But that kind of stupid feud can go on forever, and I had promised.

As I walked out on the porch, she gave me a worried, hesitant look.

"Are you still angry with me?" she asked.

"No."

"Yes, you are. I can tell," she insisted.

"No, I'm not, but I have something to tell you. I'm going into Provincetown again to see our friend Terry, but I think I should go alone. He might be more willing to talk to me if I'm alone."

"Are you sure you're not doing this because you're mad?"

I patted her arm. "Take my word for it."

She gave a bright smile of relief. "Okay, but you'll tell me everything that happens?"

"You've got my guarantee."

"I'll hold you to it," she said.

I reached The Leather Place by five forty-five. Since the shop closed at six and was probably empty most of the time anyway, I figured there was a good chance of getting Terry alone. Before going in I took a quick walk down the side alley and around the back of the shop. Sure enough, in the small parking lot there sat a little red sports car. Things were starting to make sense. Seeing the car made me feel so good that even the sight of Terry's sneering face as he came through the beaded curtain at the back of the shop didn't bother me.

"Well, if it isn't Lou. I thought you'd be on the beach with Jessie, keeping her warm."

I still felt good enough to resist the impulse to smash in his face, so all I said was, "I just stopped by to make sure you had gotten my message."

"What message is that?" he asked cautiously.

"The one I asked Sandy to give you," I answered, casually running my hand over some belts that looked like giant dog collars.

"Sandy. When did you meet her?" he asked, appearing genuinely confused.

"Yesterday. Didn't she tell you?"

"I guess she forgot," Terry said, regaining his smile. "What was the message?"

I ignored him as though it weren't important and went on examining the belts. As craftsmanship, they were a good argument for machine-made goods.

"C'mon, Lou, what was it?" Now he was trying to be friendly. It was a strain for him.

"It was about David's death," I said, pausing for effect. Terry licked his lips like a little kid looking at an ice-cream cone, and the beady piggish eyes bugged even farther out of his head.

"What about it?"

"Not much. Just that someone saw David on the cliffs that afternoon, and he wasn't alone."

I watched Terry's face closely. There certainly were reactions, but they weren't the ones I had expected. I thought for sure that Terry had been with David that day, maybe had argued with him and had purposely or accidentally pushed him over the edge. But the expression on his face wasn't guilt or fear, it was greed. He gave a huge smile, showing all of his bad teeth, rubbed his hands together and emitted a chuckle as if he finally had someone exactly where he wanted him. I felt sorry for whoever it was.

"Lou, you'll never know what a favor you've done for me," he said, his head bobbing up and down like a crazy puppet. "Is there anything I can do for you? Something in leather at half price?"

"Forget it," I said in disgust.

"I'll do just that. Now it's time to close, and I have things to do. So you'll have to get out."

Trying to seem cool, as though I understood everything, I strolled out slowly. But I could hear him laughing even louder behind me as I left.

I had parked down in the public lot by the beach again. As I turned off of Commercial Street and began walking toward the ocean, a black limousine pulled up in front of me and a tall heavyset man with dark wavy hair jumped out quickly and blocked my way.

"Please get into the car," he said with a slight accent. Looking into his dark, unblinking eyes, I knew I didn't have a choice.

I slid into the back seat of the car, and he closed the door. The heavily tinted glass of the windows gave the interior of the car a cool, shadowy appearance, and it was a moment before my eyes adjusted enough for me to see the guy sitting across from me. A dark-complexioned man in a white suit, who could have been anywhere from thirty to fifty, sat there patiently waiting for my eyes to focus on him. His small plump hands rested on the folding desk in front of him, and he studied me with a curious little smile.

"What's going on here? Who are you?" I asked nervously.

"You may call me Mr. Ramirez," he answered softly.

"Is that your name?"

"Sometimes it is. And you are . . ."

"Lou Dunlop. What do you want?"

"I couldn't help but notice that you have recently twice visited a shop that I own."

"What shop?"

"The Leather Place."

"I thought Terry McCoy ran it."

"He is my employee," Mr. Ramirez said, rearranging his plump hands on the desk. I had the feeling that he rarely moved more than was absolutely necessary, conserving his energy until it was needed. I didn't want to be around when that time came.

"Why did you visit him?"

"I'm staying with David Marshal's family, so I wanted to ask Terry some questions."

"About what?"

I hesitated briefly. "About David Marshal's death."

"I believe the newspapers reported that it was a tragic accident."

I shrugged.

"Perhaps you are wondering why I keep such a close watch on my places of business?" he asked, changing the subject. I didn't say anything, and he went on. "In this line of work, one must be careful to insure the quality of one's product and to encourage one's employees to follow company policy very carefully."

His eyes took on a dreamy look, and he held his hands open in front of him in sort of a phony pleading gesture. "Sometimes employees decide to take too much initiative, then they must be reprimanded. Sometimes severely."

"What kind of business are you in?" I asked.

"Importing."

"What do you import?"

"What do you think?" he asked quickly.

"Leather?" I answered just as quickly.

"That is a good answer," he said with a satisfied smile.

"Did David fail to follow company policy?" I was starting to sound just like Ramirez.

Ramirez's eyes narrowed, and the smile disappeared from his face. "If I thought you were asking whether I had had David Marshal killed, that would be a very dangerous question—dangerous for you." He gave a short laugh and rubbed his hands on the desk. "But no, I do not know how David came to die."

"Why are you watching Terry so closely?" I asked.

"No more questions!" he said sharply, and then suddenly relaxed. The smile returned. "I invited you. You are my guest and will answer my questions."

I nodded. The two men in the front seat on the other side of the glass partition continued to stare straight ahead.

"Why do you think that David's unfortunate death was anything other than the terrible accident it was reported to be?" Ramirez asked.

"Because someone was with him when he fell."

Ramirez raised a short, thick index finger up next to his nose. For him that was virtually a jump of surprise.

"Who was with him?"

"I don't know," I replied.

"Ah!"

"Ah, what?" I felt like asking, but kept my mouth shut.

"And you think that it may have been Terry?" he asked.

"Possibly."

"It was not, of that I can assure you. Terry was in the shop that afternoon and did not go to meet David on the beach."

"You were watching him?"

Ramirez nodded slightly.

"Louis, I would advise you not to visit The Leather Place again or to attempt to contact Terry McCoy. There are elements of this situation that you do not understand and could not possibly concern you."

I looked at him without indicating whether I agreed or not.

"In case you are wondering what will happen if you ignore my instructions, let me assure you that it will not be pleasant." His left hand moved with surprising speed to a button near the door handle. The guy with the wavy hair jumped out and opened the door.

"Goodbye, Louis," said Mr. Ramirez without glancing in my direction.

I climbed out quickly. The fellow with the wavy hair got in the front, and the limousine smoothly slid away.

I felt as if I had just been beaten up on the inside, in a way that didn't leave any bruises on your body but left plenty on your mind.

## *Chapter Eleven*

On the way back from Provincetown I stopped at a small restaurant along the side of the highway. It wasn't because I was particularly hungry, but I needed to sit down somewhere and try to stop the flip-flops my stomach had been doing ever since my conversation with Ramirez. It turned out to be one of those places built yesterday that had been given an old nautical look by hanging fish nets, anchors and ships' wheels on walls made out of phony planking. It's really weird to think about, but somewhere out there are people making all this fishing gear for walls, knowing the only water the stuff will ever come near is what's in the glass on your table.

Munching on greasy fish and chips, I wondered where I had gone wrong. The way Terry had acted suggested that he hadn't been with David that afternoon, and even though Ramirez was a hood, I sort of believed what he had said about Terry being in the shop when David died. But Terry had also seemed to have some idea who had been with David. Another problem was that if Terry hadn't gotten my message about David possibly being murdered until today, then who had been following me around like a shadow?

The more I thought about it, the more it all came back to the same point: I still didn't know enough about David. Molly had told me a few things that showed he wasn't perfect, but who would tell me more unpleasant items. The answer came to me in a flash—a former girlfriend. A girl who had just split with him would have plenty to say. If I went to see Carolyn Hayes in the morning, there might be enough to break this whole thing wide open before we were supposed to leave in the afternoon. Uncle Stephen would be sure to let us stay for another day if I could tell him that David had been murdered and I knew who had done it. But what if it all led back to Ramirez, a small voice in the back of my mind insisted. I tried to push the thought away by jamming another French fry in my mouth. "I'll cross that bridge when I come to it," I said aloud, and the waitress gave me a funny look.

It was dark by the time I got to the house. Looking through the living room window, I could see Molly curled on the sofa reading a book and Aunt Millie sitting in her rocking chair knitting. Jessie was most likely asleep already. Jessie had lost David, and I had lost her.

There was a full moon and a warm breeze, so I decided to walk down to the beach. As I followed the road and walked over the sand to the lower part of the cliffs, I could see clearly in the moonlight, but there weren't any colors, everything just seemed to give off a pale white glow. I was about to go down the path to the stairs that led to the beach when I heard a strange sound. It was the soft flap of birds' wings beating against the air. I turned and went slowly up the trail toward the spot from which David had fallen. I went about twenty feet, then I saw Jessie.

She was standing two steps from the edge of the cliff, gazing out at the ocean. Her arms were outstretched, and her nightgown billowed behind her as it filled with the breeze from off the water. Her eyes seemed fixed on a point far out in the sea, somewhere beyond the waves that I could hear crashing on the shore. Somewhere out beyond the moon.

The way Jessie stood, with her nightgown pressed against her body by the breeze, she looked like one of those wooden carvings of women that the old whaling ships had on their bows. Something to remind them of home and protect them from what might be coming. But this was no wooden girl. She took a step forward without looking down, as if in a trance. One more step, and she would plunge over the edge.

I crept slowly up the path until she was just beyond arm's reach, hoping with every step that she wouldn't notice me. But something must have disturbed her dream because she turned her head slightly, as though aware that someone was near.

"Life is real. Life is sweet," she sang in a high, singsong voice that sent a chill through me. Then she stopped and seemed to be listening to the waves. They must have been saying something different because she raised her right foot to take another step, one that would be out into nothingness.

It was like seeing everything in slow motion. The foot started to come down, found nothing under it, and her body slowly began to swing off balance. I leaped forward, got my right hand on her arm and pulled! For a long moment we teetered on the edge, my strength against her weight. Then we both fell away from the cliff and into the sand. Under other circumstances this would have been fun, but now she was just lying on the ground, staring up as though I wasn't there. After getting my breath I lifted her onto her feet and put my arm around her for the walk back.

This wasn't much of an improvement over our last visit to the beach, and all at once it hit me again that for a week it was like she had been in suspended animation, where nothing could get through to her. I understood how that could happen with Aunt Millie; she was an older woman and it was her son. But Jessie was a tough kid. I would have expected her to hold up better under pressure than anyone I knew, and here I was almost carrying her home for the second time in less than two weeks.

When I got Jessie inside, I put her on the sofa and explained what had happened to Aunt Millie and Molly.

"How could she have gotten out?" Aunt Millie asked, as if the most important thing was to find out who was to blame.

"She must have slipped out the back door," Molly answered. "But it doesn't matter, you'd better get in touch with Stephen."

Aunt Millie tried to call him at their house in Boston and then at the office, but there was no answer at either place. Not being able to reach him, Aunt Millie stood in front of the phone as though all she could do was keep on calling until he answered.

"Isn't there another doctor on the Cape you could call?" I asked in frustration.

Aunt Millie just stared at me.

"We had Dr. Bochman that time when I had the flu and Stephen was away on a trip," Molly said. She was sitting on the sofa next to Jessie, who was silently swaying back and forth. "He only lives a half mile away. Maybe he'll come to the house?"

"But we don't really *know* him," Aunt Millie complained.

"And you may not know your niece much longer if you don't do something," I said.

Aunt Millie stood there undecided, as though trying to figure out what Uncle Stephen would want her to do. Finally she dialed and almost apologetically explained Jessie's condition to Dr. Bochman. Apparently the doctor took the situation a lot more seriously than Aunt Millie because he said he'd be right over. A doctor who makes house calls, I thought. He must be ninety years old. I hoped that he remembered enough medicine to help Jessie.

When Molly answered the door ten minutes later, I was surprised to see a man in his late twenties dressed in jeans and a sweatshirt. He knelt down in front of Jessie, held her head steady to shine a light in her eyes, then felt her pulse.

"Let's take her upstairs," he said, looking at me.

Between the two of us we got her up the stairs and into the back bedroom. Then I left the doctor and Aunt Millie with Jessie and went to the living room.

About fifteen minutes later they came down the stairs. Aunt Millie remained standing, but the doctor put his bag down on the floor and sat on the sofa where Jessie had been.

"Your friend is suffering from a drug reaction. Does she use pills regularly?"

"No, she doesn't use any kind of drugs!"

"Are you sure?"

"Yes."

Aunt Millie coughed as if she wanted to say something.

"Well?" Doctor Bochman said, waiting for her to begin.

"Since David's death, Stephen has been giving both of us some tranquilizers to help us get through the worst. We take them first thing in the morning when we get up and just before going to bed at night. This is what they look like," Aunt Millie said, reaching in her apron pocket and then holding out her hand. In her palm was a little blue pill.

Dr. Bochman looked at it, then raised an eyebrow and said carefully, "Well, if your husband has been treating her, I don't want to interfere. But she seems to be having an acute negative response to the drug. It may be the dosage, or she might have an allergic reaction. This is a pretty powerful tranquilizer."

"Should she be taken off the pills?" I asked.

He hesitated. "Dr. Marshal will have to make that decision. I've just given her a very mild sedative. She should stay in bed until Dr. Marshal can see her and not be given any further medication. When will he be back?"

"Sometime tomorrow," Molly answered.

"But they were supposed to go home tomorrow," Aunt Millie said, as though she would be in trouble if we didn't.

The doctor sighed. "I'm not sure that Jessie shouldn't be put right in the hospital tonight for observation. If she were my patient I would. She's a sick young woman and certainly shouldn't be moved until a physician examines her tomorrow. And it might be longer than that before she can travel."

He said that in such a clear, no-nonsense tone that Aunt Millie just nodded her head once and then kept it down, staring at the floor.

"And no more pills until Dr. Marshal looks at her," Bochman added firmly.

Molly went to the door with the doctor, and I could hear them talking softly on the porch. Aunt Millie sat in her chair with her knitting on the small round table beside her. She was still staring at the floor and continued even after Molly came back into the room. Molly looked at her mother, then went over and sat on the floor at her feet. Gently she placed her head on Aunt Millie's knee. Absent-mindedly her mother reached out and stroked her hair.

Without speaking, I went upstairs. I peeked into Jessie's room. She was lying on her side and seemed to be asleep. I went along down the hall to my room. It looked as if I had another day to find out the truth, but who knew what the price would be for Jessie?

# Chapter Twelve

The change in Aunt Millie the next morning was like going from darkness into sunshine. Before I got downstairs I caught the unfamiliar aroma of eggs and toast, and in the kitchen Molly was perched on a stool chatting happily with her mother, who was working over the stove. The days of soggy, cold cereal finally seemed to be over. Hallelujah!

I walked into the kitchen and got a big cheery greeting from both of them.

"You seem to be feeling better this morning," I said to Aunt Millie.

"After what Dr. Bochman said last night, I decided not to take any pills last night or this morning, and I feel much better already."

"I wonder why Stephen had you both taking them in the first place?" asked Molly.

"I'm sure he thought it was for the best," answered Aunt Millie, "but sometimes a person who loves you underestimates how strong you are. I'm sure he only wanted to help us."

"How's Jessie?" I asked.

"She's still sleeping," said Aunt Millie, turning the eggs with a skillful flip of the wrist. "After breakfast I'll go up and sit with her until she awakens."

Breakfast turned out to be the first normal meal I'd had since my arrival. The three of us actually had a conversation instead of a memorial service. David's name wasn't mentioned once, although you could sense everyone sidestepping it, especially when Aunt Millie started talking about buying Molly new clothes before she started back to school. We were probably all thinking that David would never be starting back to anything. But even though she looked sad at times, Aunt Millie didn't cry, and she even suggested that for the last couple of days of my visit I might as well sleep in David's bed.

"I thought Jessie and I were going to leave tomorrow," I said in surprise.

"The doctor said Jessie shouldn't be moved that soon. Plus today is Thursday, and we're all going back to Boston on Sunday. It just doesn't make sense for the two of you to leave tomorrow. We'll all leave on the same day."

Then she really startled me by reaching over and poking me in the arm and saying, "And I can use somebody strong to help with the packing." For once I could see how Molly took after her mother.

After breakfast, before Aunt Millie went upstairs to stay with Jessie, she suggested that we go out for a swim or a drive.

As soon as the door closed Molly wanted to know what had happened at The Leather Place yesterday, so I explained about Terry's peculiar behavior and my conversation with Ramirez.

Molly whistled. "What do you think is going on?"

I shook my head in frustration. "I don't know yet."

"Well, since you struck out with Terry, what are we going to do today, O wise detective?"

"I think we'll visit your brother's ex-girlfriend, Carolyn Hayes."

"What do you expect to find out there?"

I gave my best man-of-the-world smile. "You never know. Guys tell their girls lots of things they wouldn't tell anyone else. She may know more about what David and Terry were up to at The Leather Place. Somehow I have the idea that's the key to this puzzle."

"Okay. All we have to do is drive over to the Bay, and this will give you a chance to see the other side of the Cape."

\* \* \*

The Hayes house was more like a mansion. It was perched on a low dune about fifty yards from the beach. Made all of metal and glass and assembled at strange angles, it looked like a clumsy space ship that had crash-landed on the sand.

There were no steep cliffs here. The beach just gradually got tired out and ran into the Bay. Right now was low tide, so a stretch of wet sand that looked to be a couple of miles wide was uncovered. When the tide came in a few hours from now, all of it would be under water at the bottom on the Bay.

The door was answered by a kid of about ten, who turned out to be Carolyn's younger brother. He was all alone in the house. The drapes were drawn over the big windows in the living room, and in the darkest corner a color television was showing a rerun of an old comedy series. The canned laughter made it sound hysterical.

Reluctantly the kid took us out on a huge side deck overlooking the Bay.

"There she is," he said, pointing to a small figure walking on the sand about half a mile offshore. Glancing back inside at the television so as not to miss anything, he said, "She likes to pick up shells and things when the tide is out." He shrugged as though to say that this was typically strange behavior for an older sister.

We thanked him and went down the stairs from the deck to the shore. We took off our shoes and began to walk out on the wet sand uncovered by the tide. Little pools of water remained in gullies with small fish swimming in them, waiting for the ocean to come back and free them.

When we had almost reached Carolyn, I said to Molly, "After you introduce us, maybe you should, um, take a walk for a few minutes and leave us alone to talk."

"Why? I thought there were no more secrets! This Lone Ranger routine is getting to be a bore."

"Look, there are things she may not want to tell me in front of you. Don't worry, I'll tell you everything. I told you all about my talk with Terry, didn't I?"

Molly grunted. "Okay, but you better tell me everything."

"Sure."

"Hi, Molly," Carolyn called when Molly waved to her.

As we got nearer I saw that she was a pretty girl with dark hair and a nice figure that wasn't covered up too much by her two-piece suit. Maybe her eyes were a little close together and the long face gave her a slightly horsey look, but who am I to be fussy?

She seemed embarrassed for a moment, then said, "Molly, I was very sorry to hear about David. It was a terrible accident and must have been an awful shock for your family."

Molly thanked her, then introduced me. "Lou wants to know a little more about what David was like and thought that maybe you could help him."

"Why do you want to know about him?" she asked, staring in toward shore as though it might offer a chance to escape my questions.

I gave Molly a meaningful glance, and grudgingly she started to wander off toward a large pool of water several yards farther out.

Turning back to Carolyn, I said, "I never met David, and I've heard so much about him that I wondered what he was really like."

"That's not much of a reason. You'll have to do better than that." She stooped down and picked up a stone, almost completely black and worn smooth. "If you tell me the truth, maybe I'll give you some information, as long as you don't spread it around."

"Okay, someone was with David when he fell. Someone who may have pushed him or left him to die. I'm just trying to find out if he knew any people like that."

She stood very still for a moment. "Do you really think something like that happened?"

I nodded.

Carolyn gave a big sigh. "David probably knew lots of people who could do a thing like that. Maybe he could even do it himself. But you know—" she paused for a moment "—he had a real sweet smile, knew all the right words and had a way of making you feel like you were something special. If somebody did that to him, they should get paid back."

She started walking again, not looking up from the sand. I kept in step next to her.

"But I don't think he knew many people around here," she went on. "He'd only just come back from California."

"What about Terry McCoy?"

"Funny you should ask," she said without a smile. "He's the one guy who could have done it, but he had more to gain by having David alive."

"Why?"

"Have you ever seen The Leather Place?"

"Yeah."

"Well then, you know that nobody is making any money selling those junky belts and watchbands. It's the little sideline that makes the rent money."

"What sideline?" I asked slowly, but a sinking feeling in my stomach told me I had already guessed.

"Drugs. Terry is a pretty well-known dealer, and he took David in with him this summer."

I gazed out at a large half-sunken freighter on the horizon. It seemed as though you could keep on walking right out to it. I wondered what would be inside. Probably nothing as bad as this.

"Why did Terry take David on as a partner?" I asked.

"If you've met Terry, you know that most people would want to take a shower after just talking to him. But David had charm, and could he sell." Her smile slipped a little, and she bent down to pick up a shell, but it was broken so she tossed it away. "Plus they had some kind of special deal going."

"What sort of deal?"

"I never really knew, but David said once that he could get all the money they would need to expand the business because he knew something about somebody."

"What did he know?"

"All he ever said was that it would expose a real phony."

We turned and headed toward where Molly was wading in a tidal pool. The sun was warm on the side of my face, and the feel of the wet sand under my feet was cool. A couple of real little kids were chasing an inflated raft that was blowing away from them in the breeze. They would be lucky to ever catch it.

Carolyn stopped before we reached Molly. "I think I'll stay here," she said. "Say goodbye to Molly for me. And I hope you find out what happened to David if it means so much to you."

I thanked her and started to walk away but turned back after a few steps. "By the way, is that why you broke up with David, you found out about the drugs?"

"I wish. He broke up with me. He wanted me to make some drug deals with the kids down at the yacht club. I said, 'C'mon, David, that really is asking too much. That's really tacky.' He never said a thing, he didn't argue. He only smiled, gave a wave and I never saw him again."

With a quick awkward movement she bent over to examine some stones. When I looked back a second later, I saw her hand sneak up to wipe away the tears.

## Chapter Thirteen

Molly walked back to shore alongside me, not asking any questions but obviously anxious for me to begin. What was I supposed to do? Explain as gently as possible that her beloved brother had been a real sweet guy, who by next year would have had her peddling joints in the girls' room or worse?

"Carolyn thinks that Terry was selling drugs," I began cautiously.

"That's no big surprise," she said calmly, but then its significance dawned on her and she paused, "Does that mean that David was involved?"

"It doesn't mean it," I said, continuing to walk, so she had to rush to catch up.

"So then maybe Terry killed him because he wouldn't go along with dealing drugs. He got David to meet him out on the cliffs and then pushed him over," she said excitedly.

We got in the car, and I started up the engine. Before I could put it in gear, she reached over, turned the engine off and pulled the keys out of the ignition. She held them out the window in her right hand.

"The truth, Lou, all of it. Don't treat me like a kid, or we'll sit here all afternoon. And if you try to get the keys away from me, I'll throw them so far out into the sand that you'll never find them."

Her face was bright red, and she looked ready to cry. I sat and felt the sweat run down my back and form a pool when it reached the waistband of my pants. On the beach in front of us, two guys were playing with a small dog. One of them would throw a red ball, and the dog would run into the surf and bring it back to them. Every once in a while, one of the guys only pretended to throw the ball. The dog would rush out into the water, waiting for the ball to fall. When it didn't come down, the dog would look back with a trusting, expectant expression at its master, who pretended to throw it again. After a couple of false throws, the dog refused to turn around and simply stood there as if to say, "I'm ready to get down to business whenever you're through playing silly games." I knew that eventually Molly and I would reach the same point.

"Okay, I don't think David was exactly opposed to what Terry was doing."

"Don't beat around the bush. There's not much about David that I wouldn't believe. He may have been my brother, but I knew what he was like."

So I gave in and told her pretty much what Carolyn had said, leaving out the blackmail part.

Molly returned the keys. "You know it's not really that outrageous. Lots of kids, even ones my age, sell drugs to pick up a little extra money. But poor David, everything he tried he had to do in a big way."

"Maybe he shouldn't have majored in business."

Molly's eyes grew wide. "Maybe it was a mob hit! You know, like on television, maybe David and Terry were muscling in on someone else's turf."

"I think we're jumping to conclusions," I said, trying to sound calm. "They would have taken out Terry and Ramirez, too, if that were the case."

Molly grinned at me. "Why are you so afraid of the mob? Detectives on television aren't afraid."

"That's because they know they'll be back next week. I don't have that guarantee."

Molly was silent for a moment, then she said, "Well, it couldn't have been Terry who killed David. He's too greedy to do in his best salesman."

"If we could only find out what the Bottle Woman saw, then we might find out who did."

"Then let's pay her another visit this afternoon."

"Okay, but this time we'll make sure first that her little son isn't home," I said, starting the car.

"That's one of your problems, Lou, you just don't like children."

"Not when they're twice as big as I am."

It was lunchtime when we got back to the house. Uncle Stephen's car wasn't in the driveway. Aunt Millie, appearing even livelier than she had at breakfast, was cooking some soup on the stove, and cheese sandwiches were melting deliciously on the griddle.

"I'm afraid that my meals haven't been much for the past couple of weeks," she said smiling, "but starting now, things are going to improve."

We both smiled back and gave vague answers as to where we had been, having decided on the way to the house not to tell anyone about David's drug involvement until we were sure that it had to come out in order to catch his murderer.

"How's Jessie?" I asked.

"Find out for yourself," she responded, handing me a flowered tray with a bowl of soup and a sandwich on it. "She's been asking for you all morning."

I bounded up the stairs, barely managing to keep the tray balanced, and went into the corner bedroom. Jessie was sitting in the upholstered chair by the large corner window facing the ocean. She was wearing her nightgown and a robe, but her hair was combed and her eyes, which turned to me as soon as I entered the room, were bright.

"Thanks, Lou," she said as I put the tray on the small metal table in front of her.

"How are you feeling?"

"Better than I have in days. I felt so tired before and so... so indifferent."

"Well, you had a pretty rough time of it. David's death was a big shock to you."

"Yeah, I guess it was partly that, and those pills must have really knocked me out. It was like when you're sick and have a high fever. Everything seems far away, and you can't pay attention to anything for long. Life is just out of focus."

I nodded and took her hand.

"I hear that I took a little stroll last night," she said with that old sly Jessie grin. "I could have gotten a chill out there. Thanks for bringing me back, Lou."

It could have been the big chill, Jes, the one you don't come back from, I thought.

"Lean over," she said. When I did she gave me a soft kiss on the lips. "We have a lot of lost time to make up for."

I sat there with the biggest smile on my face that I'd had in weeks.

# *Chapter Fourteen*

Somehow the Bottle Woman's shack seemed different, even lonelier and less homey if that was possible. Finally I realized that the pathetic curtain that had covered the rat hole of a window was gone. It's those little touches that make a house a home, along with some warmth and happiness.

There had been plenty of both over lunch, which had been a rerun of breakfast with Aunt Millie cheerfully discussing the new school year with Molly. Her mood only faltered once when I asked where Uncle Stephen was. Apparently, he had called in the morning to say that an emergency would keep him in Boston all day. When Aunt Millie explained about

Dr. Bochman's visit and Jessie's problem, he had been very concerned, but couldn't promise to be home before evening. Even though Jessie seemed fine, we were all disappointed that she couldn't be examined sooner.

Molly walked up to the door of the Bottle Woman's house and knocked, but no one answered.

"Here we go again," she said, turning the handle and starting to open the door.

"Oh no we don't!" I said, grabbing her arm. "Let me take a look in the window first. I don't want to stumble in on King Kong again."

"I can handle him," she protested as I pulled her away from the door and around to the window.

An old plastic milk rack was leaning against the wall, and I was able to balance myself on it and reach the window. The dirt on the glass was so thick that I had to spit on my handkerchief and rub for several seconds before I could see inside. There wasn't much to see. The place was empty! Not a bottle, can, bin, cot or giant was in sight.

We went around to the door and walked inside. I could see the newspaper ad now: "Ocean front shack for rent, security deposit required." Either by themselves, but more likely with some kind of help, the two of them had moved on—completely. Only the foul, sweet smell of old soda and a few flies who had lost their meal ticket remained behind.

"Looks like they took off," I said, stepping outside for some fresh air.

"Who's that?" Molly asked, pointing up the path. It was the figure in black. He had just stopped his bicycle in the middle of the road and was staring down at us. I broke into a run. The rider spun the bike around and, with the rear wheel fishtailing on the sandy road, sped away.

I could never catch up by chasing him, but I knew that the road did a loop and came around on the other side of the dune in front of me. I started up at full speed. My feet sank deeply into the sand, and after a few yards the muscles in my upper legs were twisted like ropes and numb from the effort. But I forced my body forward, and by bringing my knees high, almost up to my chin, I reached the top.

He was racing along the road, coming up on my left. I had to get down the dune quickly to cut him off. I started running down the face of the dune, but my run turned into a slide, and before I knew it I was on my back riding the sand the way some people go over a waterfall.

It was pure luck that the dune threw me out on the road just as the bicycle was racing past. The right handlebar caught me in the stomach, knocking the wind out of me, and I collapsed across the bike. The rider and I both sprawled onto the road, and I think I actually heard my own head bounce as it hit the pavement.

I must have blacked out for a moment. When I woke up I felt the hot pavement and some grains of sand under the right side of my face that seemed about the size of boulders. I rolled over on my back and saw the dark figure standing above me blocking out the sun. I didn't know whether to cry or scream, so I simply lay there catching my breath and trying to blend into the background.

A hand reached down to me. "Need some help up?" a soft voice asked.

I grabbed the hand and pulled myself to my feet. Now I could make out a face.

"Sandy?"

"Actually, it's Sergeant Felden," she said, flashing a police ID she had taken from her back pocket.

"Did the department run out of squad cars?"

She smiled and picked up the bike. "I had half a day off, so I thought I'd combine business and recreation by riding out to see Mrs. Rosewell again. It turned out to be more exciting than I expected. Are you okay? Any dizziness or nausea?"

"No more than usual. Who's Mrs. Rosewell?"

"The old woman who collects the empties. When you strolled into The Leather Place and dropped that bombshell about someone being with David when he died, I had to find out where you'd gotten your information. You spotted me when I followed you out here, so I had to come back a few hours later to question her. You know, you really upset her son."

"Only dynamite could do that. What did you find out?"

"Nothing more than you did. She saw somebody with David that day, but was too far away to make out who it was. I kept hoping she could link his death with Terry; that's why I never passed on your message to him. Terry was pretty suspicious after your second visit when I told him I'd simply forgotten to mention it."

"So that was your red car in back of the shop, and you were working undercover at The Leather Place. What are you trying to do, nail Terry for dealing drugs?"

"You found out about that, too," she said in surprise. "Yeah, we've been after him for a while. He's not really big time, but big enough to be a problem."

"What about Ramirez?"

Sandy stared. "What do you know about him?" she gasped.

I explained about our friendly chat in the back of his car.

"Now he really *is* big time," said Sandy. "He's a major drug importer from South America. I thought he might be Mr. Big, but I couldn't be sure. Terry never mentioned his name."

"How did David fit into all this?"

Sandy hesitated a moment and bit her lip. "Officially he didn't. Our operation only started after I moved into his job, but we checked out his background. Although he had never been charged, the police in California had questioned him in a couple of drug probes near San Diego. Terry told me that David had come to him and asked to make some deliveries and set up a few sales. Kind of an apprenticeship, I guess, but they had big plans for the future.''

"What kind of plans?"

"All I know is that after Terry saw you and found out that someone had been seen with David on the cliffs, he made a phone call and got real happy. He kept clapping his hands and saying, 'Maybe it will work after all.' I don't think he had anything to do with David's death, but he sure thinks he knows who did."

"Maybe we can get it out of him. Why don't you threaten to arrest him unless he talks?"

Sandy shook her head. "This whole operation is aimed at catching the person behind him. We want to grab Terry making a big buy from his supplier."

"Ramirez?"

"Probably. So I can't move against him now. It would ruin everything."

"Great," I said softly. "Just when I thought I was getting close to an answer to this thing, it slips away."

Sandy put her hand on my arm. "Lou, there might not be an answer. Maybe David's death was only an accident. The old woman could have been wrong."

Molly came down the road toward us. She was exhausted, half running and half walking. Her face was red and sweat stood out on her forehead.

"Are you all right?" she called out.

I nodded, and then she recognized Sandy.

"You!" she cried. "I was suspicious of you from the start. Somebody like you working at The Leather Place—fat chance!"

"I'm glad Terry isn't as smart as you are," said Sandy with a smile.

I explained who Sandy was and why she was working for Terry. Molly seemed interested but not inclined to forgive Sandy for deceiving us.

"One thing," I said to Sandy, "why did you keep following me even after you found the Bottle Woman?"

She shuffled her feet and said carefully, "You're talking about that time you saw me on the cliff while you were swimming."

"Yeah, and probably lots of other times when I didn't see you."

"Well, I thought that maybe you were trying to blackmail Terry, and I was afraid he might try to shut you up. I was only keeping an eye on you for your own protection."

"Blackmail! You thought I would do that?"

"Yeah, she thought I was along for muscle," Molly added accusingly.

"You have to admit that what you told me at the shop sounded like a warning to Terry," Sandy said.

"Okay, but why did you have to push me into the garbage that night, and what were you doing trying to break into the house?"

Sandy looked confused, and after I explained she shook her head. "That wasn't me."

"Then who was it?" I asked no one in particular.

"Probably Jack the Ripper," said Molly in disgust. "He must be involved in this mess somewhere."

## Chapter Fifteen

On the way back we stopped off at a supermarket because Molly had to pick up some things for Aunt Millie. Since it was the middle of a beautiful beach afternoon, very few people were in the store, and we were able to cruise up and down the aisles. As we went by the fruit, Molly squinted at her list, and said we needed a few oranges. Without thinking, I grabbed a plastic bag and pulled an orange out of the middle of the large pile on the counter next to me. It was an orange avalanche! There seemed to be hundreds of them streaming between my desperate hands and landing with a dull *thunk* on the floor.

"Let's get out of here. We can come back later, and no one will know we did it," I said urgently.

"C'mon, Lou, why don't we just pick them up," said Molly, bending over and beginning to toss them on the counter.

Reluctantly I started to help her, while looking around every time I straightened up to see if we had been spotted. The third time I came up for air, a stock boy was walking down the aisle. You could have driven a truck between his bow legs, and he wore a price gun on his hip like he had just stepped out of a bad Western.

"Hey, you two! What are you doing over there?" he bellowed.

"We're picking up some oranges we accidentally knocked over," said Molly, explaining the obvious.

He came closer and gave a self-important yelp. "I spent two hours piling those up and a couple of clowns like you knock it all down in a second."

"Sorry," said Molly, "but we'll put them back."

"It won't be the same," he said sullenly, resting his hand on the price gun. Maybe he was going to draw and stamp us both "2/99."

"We'll do the best we can," Molly promised.

"Some of those are probably bruised," he went on as if he hadn't heard. "You're going to have to buy those."

Enough was enough. I stood up and hefted a large orange in my hand.

"Why don't you go to the other end of the aisle and squeeze a grape?" I suggested, looking at the orange and then staring at a point in the center of his forehead.

Slowly his eyes moved from the orange to my face and then back again. He started to backpedal down the aisle. "You better make sure that everything is back the way it was," he threatened as he backed into a crate of cantaloupes and almost fell.

"You see why I wanted to leave them?" I asked as I returned to helping Molly.

"It wouldn't have been dignified to run away," she replied.

I grunted and bent down to pick up the last batch.

Molly was silent during the short drive to the house, but as we pulled into the driveway she burst out, "It doesn't make sense. If Terry wasn't the one with David that afternoon, then who was?"

"That's assuming someone else was there," I said, echoing Sandy. "The Bottle Woman could have been wrong."

"Yeah, but Terry suspected someone, probably the guy David was going to squeeze money out of."

"Could be."

"Or maybe it had nothing to do with blackmail. It might have been Carolyn. You know what they say about the fury of a woman scorned."

"What do they say?" I asked with a grin.

"That it's bad news. And if you keep teasing me, you're going to find out about it."

I tried to more serious. "I guess it could have been Carolyn, but she would have to be quicker and stronger than I think she is."

Molly frowned and slumped in the seat. She pulled her lower lip over the upper in a thoughtful pout. "If only we knew what the secret was that David was going to tell me or could find that clipping. Do you think Terry has it?"

"No, if he did, he wouldn't have had to wait for my message about the other person on the cliff to start his blackmail."

"Then who does have it?" she grumbled.

"You know, David doesn't sound like the kind of guy who would put all his eggs in one basket. When it came to business, he was clever. Don't you think he would have made a copy of any important clippings he had?"

"Maybe, but Mom's been through all his stuff. It's not there."

"Well, something that's black and white and red all over isn't always easy to find," I said, trying to cheer her up. She didn't smile.

We went inside, having agreed not to mention Terry's drug involvement to Aunt Millie or Jessie since it would only raise unpleasant questions about David. Funny, I started out wanting to find out all the bad things about David, so I could show him up to Jessie. But the bad turned out to be so bad that now I was trying to hide it from her. Even though it was the truth, I didn't think that telling her would make her like me more.

By suppertime Jessie was feeling so good that Aunt Millie let her out of bed to join us, and after supper she convinced Aunt Millie that she was strong enough to take a short walk with me. We strolled on the path along the cliffs holding hands and, without either of us saying a word, ended up at the spot from which David had fallen. Off to our left the sun was sinking into the ocean and deep red light streaked the gray clouds that ran along the edge of the horizon.

"I'll miss him, Lou," Jessie said in a quiet voice, "even though we only spent that one summer together. He was nice to me when he didn't have to be. I was a skinny thirteen-year-old, who was shy, kind of strange and afraid most of the time."

"Afraid of what?"

Jessie looked out over the water and gave a deep sigh. Then she took my hand and kissed it.

"Of the ocean, of other people, of not being liked, of being myself, you name it. If he hadn't been nice to me, I don't know what would have happened. Do you understand?"

"I think I do," I answered, squeezing her hand. "He could see the kind of woman you were going to become."

"Thanks," she said with sort of a shy smile, then her eyes got a faraway look. "After that summer, I always thought about him whenever things got rough at home or at school. How he would smile at me when I told him some problem. How he would listen, then tell me everything would work out if only I believed in myself. How, when I would go on too long about something, he'd muss my hair and we'd go in for another swim, splashing around like a couple of seals in the sun."

"Why didn't you write to him or phone or visit after that summer?"

"David told me he wasn't much of a letter writer when I asked him at the end of the summer if I could write to him. And I couldn't very well call and spend most of my time speaking only to him. The whole family would have thought that I had a thing for my cousin."

"They probably did anyway."

"You're always so blunt, Lou," she said with a small grin, "and you're probably right. But I thought I was being so cool that no one would ever guess."

"And then a year later he moved out to California and didn't come back?"

"Not until this year, so I never got to see him again until this summer." She bit her lip and blinked quickly. "At least I almost did. I only wish that I had come out a week earlier. Then I would have gotten to see him and maybe even prevented his death."

"You can't know that. And remember, he would have wanted you to get through this problem the same way you got through all the others: by believing in yourself and sticking it out," I said. What I really wanted to shout was that the best thing that ever happened to you was not meeting him again. Either you would have seen him for what he had become or you wouldn't have, and either way you would have been hurt. But I didn't say any of that.

"I guess you're right," she said finally.

"Sure, remember, life is real, life is sweet."

She gave me a puzzled look as though I were quoting a saying she had heard a long time ago. "Lou, you are more than a bit strange, but I think you are exactly what I need right now."

With a laugh that was almost as good as her old ones, she grabbed my arm, and we walked to the house. But before we went in, she said, "You know, it was a little like you and Molly."

"What was?"

"David and I."

"Huh? Now wait a minute!"

"Maybe I've been sick, but it only took me a day to see that she's got a giant crush on you. So be careful."

"You're imagining things," I said, feeling excited and worried at the same time.

"Have it your own way," she said with a smug smile.

When I went up to bed, Aunt Millie reminded me that I could use the big bed instead of the roll-out; and since my back was starting to ache from sleeping on a mattress about as thick as a pancake, I decided to take advantage of it.

Maybe it was the shock of being too comfortable, or maybe I was thinking about the last thing Jessie had said, but the little illuminated bedside clock said 12:00 midnight, and I was still rolling around wide awake. It was a double bed, and I had been sleeping on the side toward the window, so I figured that maybe the breeze coming through the thin white curtains might be disturbing me. With a heave I flopped over to the other side of the bed.

No better. My mind just wouldn't let me sleep. And, to top it off, now when I tossed the bed made a crackling sound like when you crinkle plastic food wrap. What next! I looked inside the pillowcase. Nothing strange was in there. I hit the pillow a few times. It didn't make a sound. It seemed to be the mattress that was the culprit. Maybe it was that stupid little tag they put on the end of them that you're not supposed to remove "under penalty of law." When I was a small kid I cut one off and waited to see if the police would come—the start of my life of crime. I'd cut this one off, too, if it would help me sleep.

I got out of bed and pulled off the bottom sheet. There was nothing there, but when I pushed on the mattress it crackled again. So I pulled the end of the mattress off the springs and unzipped the mattress cover. I reached inside and felt paper, too much paper for a tag. Carefully I pulled it out. There were three sheets folded over. Holding the top page under the light, I could see that it was a photocopy of a short newspaper article. The other two sheets were more copies of the same thing.

I sat on the bed and read the story. Not until I finished did I realize my hands were shaking and my heart was trying to jump into my throat. A couple of deep breaths and they were seminormal again. I heard the side door shut, and Uncle Stephen's heavy tread came up the stairs. I knew that tomorrow I would have to tell him about this; it was more than I could keep to myself.

## Chapter Sixteen

I was trying to keep my eyes closed as the waves rolled me back and forth. Maybe I was lying on the bottom of the sea, and this was what it was like to be drowned. But would I be able to hear anything if I were dead? An interesting question. And I could definitely hear something now. Someone was shouting, "Wake up! Wake up!" Didn't they know you couldn't disturb the dead? I carefully opened one eye expecting to see fish and seaweed, but there was only Molly looking exasperated.

"C'mon, Lou, stir those bones. Sandy's on the phone and wants to talk to you."

"Who?"

"Sandy Felden. Sergeant Sandra Felden—the cop—the fuzz—the narc. She wants to talk to you, like right now."

"Okay. I'll be down in a second. Now get out of here," I mumbled. Reluctantly Molly left the room. I rolled out of bed and glanced at the clock. Only six. What could be that important?

I went down to the living room. No one but Molly was up yet. She was slouched on the sofa with a book and gave me a look as I went over to the phone.

"Hello?"

"This is Sandy. You'd better brace yourself."

"Why?"

"We found Terry McCoy's body on the beach this morning."

"His body?" I asked, not quite following. "You mean he's dead?"

"They don't get any deader. Somebody put a bullet through the back of his head and left him on the beach. A crazy guy who walks his dachshund at five in the morning found the body and called us."

"Any idea who did it?"

"A pretty good idea who, but not much of an idea why."

"Who?"

"Your friend Ramirez. It has all the earmarks of a mob hit with the body left in a conspicuous place to serve as a warning. But I don't know what Terry could have done that would get him killed."

Sandra's last remark was made in a sad voice, so I asked, "Did you like Terry?"

"No," she said quickly. "I don't think anyone other than his mother could *like* him. But I'd kind of gotten used to being around him, and this was a shock. It really messes up our investigation. Do you have any idea why anyone would want to kill him?"

"I'll get back to you later maybe," I said, hanging up. I noticed my hand was shaking.

I told Molly what had happened, swore her to secrecy and, before her surprise could turn to questions, went upstairs to get dressed. I sat on the bed with one sock on and one off staring into space. Terry had been blackmailing the person he thought killed David. Now he was dead. The obvious conclusion was that his victim had killed him. But he had been shot to death mob style, and if my hunch was right, the person he was blackmailing was anything but a hood. How did it all fit together? I worried about it all the way back downstairs.

Aunt Millie, Jessie and Molly spent breakfast planning how they would go about packing and finishing all the last minute chores that had to be done before returning to Boston tomorrow. I tried to listen, and nod when anyone looked directly at me or asked my opinion, but I could tell from Jessie's curious expression that I wasn't doing a very good job of hiding my concern with other things.

Uncle Stephen wasn't doing much better. Aunt Millie had to ask him twice if he was going to store the porch furniture in the cellar or in the garage. When she asked him if he wanted to examine Jessie this morning, he smiled, shook his head and said that she seemed fine. Hardly a professional medical opinion.

Molly surprised us all by pointedly asking why he had given Jessie the tranquilizers in the first place. Uncle Stephen blushed a little. He said that he hadn't realized she would have any problems, and it was probably best that she and Millie had stopped taking them now. Molly appeared disappointed with the answer but didn't say anything more.

I tried to get Uncle Stephen alone, but it was impossible in the morning because he and Aunt Millie went out to run errands. I spent the time helping Jessie and Molly clean, although they both decided that I was more of a hindrance than a help and finally sent me out to the garage to straighten out the porch furniture.

It was late afternoon, and I had just about given up hope of getting Uncle Stephen aside in a subtle way when the perfect opportunity came. He asked if anyone would like to go down to the beach for a final swim of the season. The women were all in the midst of packing clothes and said that maybe they would go later, so he and I headed to the beach alone.

I'd wanted to talk to him all day, but now that I had the chance, it was hard to begin. I kept hearing the words and seeing what his expression would be, and I couldn't get started.

We threw our rolled-up towels on the sand and stripped off our shirts. He ran into the surf first, but I was right behind him. It was a bit colder than before, but this time I tried to keep up with him as he swam out to sea. I was even with him stroke for stroke for about thirty yards, but then his more professional style began to make a difference as I lost strength. Gradually he took a large lead, so I gave up and slowly headed to shore. He continued swimming farther and farther out. For a while I could see his arms lifting rhythmically like pistons to push back the sea, then all I could make out was the dark blur of his body on the blue surface. After a few minutes the blur got larger and larger as he returned to the shore in the same methodical way.

He walked out of the water and stood for a moment before reaching down for the towel. He was breathing deeply with an occasional ragged gasp that showed that this had been quite a workout even for him.

"With a bit of practice you could be a good swimmer," he said, drying off.

"Yeah, but I haven't had the kind of opportunities you got in California."

He stopped rubbing his head with the towel and gave me a careful glance as if he was trying to remember whether he had told me about being from California. He must have remembered he had because he smiled and finished drying his hair.

"You could always go to the YMCA or somewhere with a pool. It isn't as much fun as the ocean, but it's easier to develop style and stamina doing laps."

"Well, nobody could deny that you've got both of those," I said, "but what you ran out of is luck. You know what they say: be both good and lucky, but if you can only be one, be lucky." I knew I was talking too much, but if I stopped, I wouldn't have the guts to go on.

Uncle Stephen was looking at me with patient curiosity, so I took one of the photocopies out of the pocket of my sweatshirt and handed it to him. He read it, but except for a slight tightening of the muscles in his jaw, you would have thought he was reading the sports page. But I knew he was reading about an intern, Dr. Stephen Marshal, at Los Angeles Municipal Hospital, who had been charged with beating his eight-month-old daughter. His wife had notified the social welfare department that she had seen him striking her. Trial had been scheduled for mid-April. A second, smaller article copied on the same page said that Dr. Stephen Marshal had pleaded guilty and been given a one-year suspended sentence on the condition that he undergo weekly counseling for that year.

"Where did you find this?" he asked with admirable calm.

I explained about the rustling bed. "I guess you thought you were safe once you took the clipping book from his room. What was David trying to do, blackmail you?"

"Yes," he said matter-of-factly, as though sons did this to their stepfathers every day. "He told me about the clipping a week after he came here. Actually, he'd come upon it by accident six months ago while doing some research on advertising in back issues of the *L.A. Times*." Uncle Stephen gave a short laugh. "You were right in what you said before, I didn't have much luck."

"So you stole the book and took out the clipping. Why did you return the scrapbook?"

"I didn't realize it meant so much to Millie. When she got so upset, I slipped it into a box of clothes in David's room and helped her find it."

"What was David going to do with the money?"

"He and Terry were going to expand their drug operations. He said Terry would make him a full partner if he could come up with some investment capital." Uncle Stephen paused. "I think he really enjoyed the idea that a psychiatrist would give him the money to sell drugs that destroy people's minds.

David was a sick boy, but I guess I never wanted to admit it to myself for Millie's sake."

"What did he threaten to do if you didn't give him the money?"

"To expose me to Millie, Molly and then to everyone in the profession who would listen. It probably would have ruined me. David could be very convincing."

I took a deep breath. "So you invited him for a walk on the cliffs, then gave him a friendly pat on the back that sent him over the edge?"

"Do you really believe I would do that?"

"No, but I didn't have you figured for a child beater, either."

"Give me a few minutes to explain the past, that will help you understand what happened two weeks ago."

He surveyed the horizon. "As you learned from this article, I was an intern when it happened. I don't know how much you've heard about medical education, but as an intern you are under immense pressure. For the first time, you're actually expected to function as a doctor, to treat people, sometimes for twelve, fourteen hours at a stretch.

"So I was tired most of the time. And Gloria, that was my first wife, didn't like being tied down. She was young, only twenty, when we married and didn't want to give up her friends and good times. Often I'd come home late at night or in the middle of the day, depending on my schedule, and our baby would be alone or with a neighbor because Gloria got bored and had to go out. One night I came home, and the baby was all alone crying. I went in to quiet her down. I'm not sure what happened. I think at first I just covered her mouth with my hand, but when that didn't stop the crying I may have shaken her a little. It couldn't have been any more than that. All I remember is that suddenly Gloria was there, screaming and pulling me away from the crib. The next day she filed a complaint saying that I was some kind of monster."

"So she turned you in. Did you split up after that?"

He nodded. "After my sentencing I had to stay in Los Angeles for counseling, and she moved north with the baby. Less than a year later they were both killed in an automobile accident. I decided to become a psychiatrist, partly because I had problems of my own. That's actually a pretty common reason for someone to enter the field." He added with a hint of self-mockery, "We try to heal ourselves and end up healing others."

"Then you moved out here, set up your practice and married Aunt Millie. And everything was fine until David stumbled on the article. Did you choose the meeting place on the cliffs?"

"No, that was his idea. He wanted somewhere private to tell me something important. I thought he wanted to talk about a problem he was having that he didn't want Millie to know about. I hoped that for once he was coming to me for help.''

"How did you sneak out there so no one saw you?"

"After breakfast I went into Boston, but I came back before lunch, parked in one of the public lots and walked up the beach to the cliffs. David was there, but it wasn't my help he wanted. He wanted twenty-five thousand dollars for keeping quiet about my past.''

"What did you say?"

"No, of course. I knew that once I started paying it would never stop. David would enjoy tormenting me too much. You should have heard him laugh when he told me where he had hidden the clipping. He said it was right there in his scrapbook, along with all the other rewarding experiences of his life. I told him I was going directly back to the house and tell Millie everything. David said that he would tell Millie first, and he tried to push past me to get to the path. I don't know why, maybe it was the arrogant sneer on his face, but I pushed him.''

"And he fell over the cliff?"

"No!" Uncle Stephen shouted, angry for the first time. "He stumbled backward and fell on the ground near the edge. Then he got up but accidentally looked down. Suddenly he swayed, and before I could reach him he fell.''

I wondered how hard Uncle Stephen had tried to reach him. "So you left him there on the beach and showed up later at the house to act surprised?"

"Try to understand me," he pleaded. "I'm not a beast. I went down to the beach, but he was already dead. There was nothing I could do. It had been an accident, and I hoped that for everyone's sake it would remain that way."

"You knew that David hadn't told anyone else about your past?"

"I didn't think he would tell anyone, even Terry, the full facts. If Terry knew, David would have to worry that he would try to cut him out and blackmail me directly. But maybe I was wrong. Terry called me at the office the night before last and said that he had some information about me that I wouldn't want made public. I arranged to meet him that night in Provincetown. That's why I wasn't in Boston when Millie called about Jessie."

"What did he have to say?" I asked.

"He didn't know any facts about my past, except that David had kept a clipping about me in his scrapbook, that was 'good for a few bucks,' as Terry put it. He had tried to steal it on the day of the funeral, but I already had it by then. He was about to break in a couple of nights later to search the downstairs when he ran into you." Uncle Stephen gave me a look that suggested that he wasn't the only one who kept secrets.

"But somehow he either knew or guessed that I had been with David when he died. Either way, I couldn't take any chances. He insisted I give him whatever I had in my wallet and that the next night I give him a supply of pills to sell."

"Did you agree?"

"Yes."

"Why were you going to let Terry blackmail you when you had refused David's attempt to do the same thing?"

"The past was only very embarrassing and might endanger my career, but this could lead to a murder charge."

"Did you give him the pills?"

"I wrote a number of prescriptions for non-existent patients and had them filled. I met Terry last night near the beach and gave him a bag with several hundred uppers in it."

"What happened then?"

"He took it and said he'd be in touch when he needed more."

"Is that all?"

Uncle Stephen nodded.

"Then how do you explain that Terry ended up on the same beach this morning with a hole in his head? Maybe you decided to handle him the same way you did David, only this time you made it look like a mob hit instead of an accidental fall from a cliff."

"Lou, I don't own a gun, and even if I did, I don't think I could kill anyone that way," he said. "Plus Terry got into a car with some other people when he left me."

"What kind of a car?"

"A large black one. It pulled up next to him when he was about a block away. Somebody got out, talked to Terry for a few seconds and he got in the car with him."

I leaned back on the sand. "Let's say you gave him a bag of pills like you claim you did and along comes his boss who catches him violating a company rule against private deals. So they kill him. It could have happened that way."

"So now we're the only ones who know about the clipping and the fact that I was there when David died?" Uncle Stephen asked hopefully.

"You and I and maybe the person who killed Terry."

## Chapter Seventeen

I won't insult you by suggesting that you are interested in blackmail," Uncle Stephen said carefully,
"but what are you going to do?"

A good question. An excellent one. I had started
by trying to find out what David had really been like,
so I could make him less of an idol for Jessie. Then
I had gotten involved in discovering how he had died.
Now I probably had the best answer that anyone
other than Uncle Stephen would ever have to that
one. And when you solve a mystery, you tell people.
Don't you?

"Tell the truth?" I said weakly.

Uncle Stephen waved his hand impatiently, back in command again. You couldn't keep him off balance for long. "What's truth? The important thing is that no one should be hurt. If you tell the police, then Millie and Molly will be miserable, and I might be accused of murder. What do you think that will do to them?"

I sat there trying to think. My head began to throb. "Yeah, but..."

"And Jessie," he went on. "What do you think knowing that David was a drug dealer, a liar and a blackmailer will do to her? She won't thank you for proving that you're a better person than he was. Every time she sees you, she'll remember that you're the person who destroyed one of her most precious memories."

"But it's all true," I almost shouted.

"Is the truth worth their happiness? Do you want to show how smart you are at the expense of other people? Let it go, Lou. Walk away and forget it."

The blood pounded in my head in rhythm with the waves. He was leaning forward like a lawyer, excited but in control, very professional and detached, who had just presented his case to the jury and is sure they are swaying his way.

Maybe if only once he had mentioned what it would mean for him personally, how he would gain, I would have acted differently. People who always talk about helping others make me nervous. I keep checking to see if they've lifted my wallet. Maybe he just reminded me too much of my old shrink, and I didn't like being treated like a patient. But most of all, I think it was the picture of Jessie on the cliffs, not knowing where she was and about to step off into oblivion.

"Stephen," I said. At the sound of his name without "uncle" in front, he sat back as though he knew he had lost. "I think happiness is real important, but people have to know the truth, too. If Molly found out the truth about you twenty years from now, do you think she'd thank me for not telling her sooner? I don't think so. She already knows about David and the drugs. Should I lie to her about the rest?"

"The consequences, Lou, think of the consequences," he argued.

"Shut up, Stephen. I don't know how much of what you told me is true. Maybe David did fall, but on the other hand, maybe you gave him a shove over. Maybe you beat your baby daughter once when you were half-crazy, but then maybe you beat her whenever you had a bad day. Maybe you accidentally let Jessie and Aunt Millie stay on those pills too long and then again maybe you purposely kept them drugged, so they wouldn't wonder about how David died until the summer was over and it was too late. I don't know."

He shook his head and started to speak but I went on. "No one but you will ever know for certain. What you say about consequences might be right, but hiding the truth makes it all just a little too easy for you. And I can't see it that way."

"So what are you going to do?" he asked in a low, tired voice.

"I won't go to the police, but I'm going to tell Molly everything. She's a good kid and smart, so if you ever start any trouble again, she'll blow the whistle on you. And if anything happens to her, I'll tell everyone who'll listen about you."

"I'm not a thug or a killer. I wouldn't hurt my family."

"I'll leave it up to Molly whether she tells anyone else, and I don't think she'll tell her mother unless it becomes necessary. But the truth will always be right there in the house with you."

Stephen frowned and looked away. After a moment he turned back. "I wish you wouldn't tell her, but I guess this is the best I can do."

I nodded. I only hoped it was the best for all of them.

## Chapter Eighteen

I don't think I heard anything at first over the roar of the waves. A small shower of sand sprang up from a little pockmark in front of Stephen's left foot, sort of the way dust rises on a dirt road when it begins to rain. Stephen got up on his knees and turned to look toward the stairs. Something that sounded like a dragonfly buzzed past my ear. I looked at Stephen. He was holding his arm where redness was already seeping through his fingers. I saw two men on the stairs. One was already halfway down the beach; the other was leaning against the railing a flight farther up and pointing something at us.

Stephen and I both scrambled to our feet. "He's got a gun!" Stephen gasped as the blood snaked down his arm and into his clenched hand.

"They're Ramirez's men," I said dully. The guy in the lead started clamoring down the last flight of stairs. Even though his legs were pumping quickly, he seemed to be coming so slowly that it was like watching a slow-motion replay. I recognized him as the one who had forced me into the car.

"Get out of here!" Stephen said urgently, without turning away from the two gunmen. "Run!"

"Run where?" All around were miles of empty beach with nowhere to hide.

Stephen spared me a quick glance. "Into the water. Get into the water and keep going," he said sharply, then turned away.

I ran a few yards into the water until it was up to my chest and stopped to look back. Stephen was still standing in the same spot facing the stairway. The first hood had reached the beach and was starting to run toward him.

"C'mon, Stephen," I shouted. If he heard me, he never let on. He just stood there with his shoulders slumped like someone waiting for a bus after a tough day at work.

The gunman stopped about twenty feet away. Even he seemed a little confused that Stephen didn't try to run. The sound of the shot sent the sea gulls wheeling into noisy flight up above the cliffs. Stephen seemed to leap into the air and do a sort of awkward somersault. A failed gymnast who landed hard on the sand and didn't move.

The second man ran past the first and bent over Stephen. Then he gestured toward me and said something to his partner, who pointed his gun in my direction. Without taking the time to turn I jumped backward into the water and started doing a fast backstroke out to sea. After about ten yards I flipped over and, taking a deep breath, began to swim underwater. I didn't know if they were shooting, but so far I hadn't been hit. At least I didn't think I had. Maybe that's one of the things you don't realize until it's too late. I wondered when Stephen had known.

I stopped to get a second wind and began to tread water. I estimated that I was about a hundred yards from shore. The two men who had chased me were staring out at the ocean, and they had been joined by a third man, short and wearing a white suit and hat. Ramirez! He handed the curly-headed man something long and thin that the guy put up to his shoulder while Ramirez pointed out at me.

*Plop* went the water about six feet to my right, and a split second later I heard the report of the rifle. I grabbed a quick breath and dived under again, swimming away from shore at an angle.

After about two minutes my lungs screamed for air. I surfaced clumsily and got a mouthful of water. The salt burned the inside of my nose as I tried to blow it out. I glanced toward shore. Ramirez had binoculars up to his eyes. He tapped the guy with the rifle on the shoulder and turned him in my direction.

Again I went under. How long could they stay on the beach before someone heard all the shooting? How long could I keep swimming around like a fish in a giant barrel before they got me with a lucky shot or, better yet for them, I got exhausted and was swept out to sea in a tragic accident. They might even try to make it look like I killed Stephen and then committed suicide. The thought startled me into opening my eyes. Green water was all around me, waiting to cut me off from air, from life.

I came up gasping. Again Ramirez spotted me, although I must have been getting harder to see on the horizon. The guy with the rifle raised it to his shoulder but suddenly stopped and turned toward the stairs. A group of figures were running down the steps, and at the top of the cliff I saw the flashing red lights of police cars.

The guy with the rifle started to point it at the police, but with a quick move Ramirez pulled it out of his hands and tossed it on the beach. The three of them waited calmly as the police approached.

Doing a slow crawl, I swam in to shore. By the time my feet reached the bottom, the police were leading Ramirez and his hoods up the stairs. Sandra splashed out into the surf and took my arm. Tiredness swept over me, and I leaned heavily on her for support.

"Are you okay, Lou?" she asked.

I nodded.

Someone who must have been a doctor was bending over Stephen. He didn't seem to be in any hurry. I guess there wasn't any reason to be. Stephen was lying on his side. There was a small hole in the front of his chest where the bullet had gone in and a much larger one, the size of a fist, where it had come out his back. A large circle of sand was already stained dark.

Sandra pulled my arm and led me toward the stairs. I leaned against the banister for a moment to rest before attempting the climb.

"How did you happen to come out here?" I asked.

"The way you talked on the phone worried me. I thought you might know something that would get you into trouble. When I stopped by the house, they told me you were here. By the time I got to the cliff, Stephen had been shot and you were playing submarine. I radioed for some help, and here we are," she concluded.

"You have a radio on your bicycle?" I asked. Somehow it seemed important to know.

Sandra looked at me strangely. "I had a patrol car this time."

I nodded as though this explained the whole situation. As I started up the steps I stumbled and caught the railing.

"Are you sure you're all right?" Sandra asked, taking my arm again. I was getting to like that.

"As all right as I'll ever be," I answered.

# *Chapter Nineteen*

A few days later Molly and I took a last walk on the beach. I explained everything. She cried a little when I showed her the newspaper articles that David had hidden, but I couldn't tell whether it was for David, for Stephen or for herself.

She hadn't cried at Stephen's funeral and had been a quiet comfort to her mother. She also hadn't asked me any questions about what led up to the shooting on the beach, taking things one step at a time, I suppose. But now Molly and I were the two people who came closest to knowing the truth.

The police thought that Terry had met secretly with Stephen for help after David's death and had told him some things that Ramirez guessed could be incriminating. So after he killed Terry he shot Stephen to play it safe and tried to include me for good measure. Ramirez couldn't very well deny it by saying he was killing a competing drug supplier who could place him at the scene of Terry's execution. The fact that Ramirez and the police were both wrong about Stephen didn't seem to matter any more.

So there things stood. Nobody had questioned how David had died, and now Stephen was just one more innocent civilian who accidentally got in the way of organized crime. Not quite the truth, but near enough to close the files. Sandra might have suspected there was more, but she was already assigned to another case with new problems.

When we reached the stairs leading up from the beach, Molly and I stopped and faced each other for that embarrassing moment before all goodbyes.

"So when it really came down to it, Lou, you told me everything. Thank you. It was more than David or Stephen did for me."

"You're welcome. It was the least I could do for my partner."

She sighed. "Poor Stephen. He never meant for any of this to happen, but he was so afraid his secret would get out. And David—well, who knows what he really wanted? Maybe he didn't even know himself."

"Yeah, I suppose it was just a case of the wrong two people ending up in the same family."

"Are you going to tell Jessie what you've told me?" Molly asked.

"No, not yet. She's been through enough. Maybe some day. If I have your permission, that is. You're the boss now."

"For once I'm in charge," she said, brightening for a moment, but then she frowned. "I'm not sure I like it."

"Welcome to the club. Are you going to tell your mother?"

Molly shook her head. "I've decided it's better if she remembers David and Stephen as she thinks they were. I don't want her to know about Stephen's past or his part, whatever it was, in David's death. It would only make her unhappy."

Her hand reached out and took mine as she said solemnly, "But you have my permission, tell Jessie everything as soon as you think she can take it. Don't make the same mistake Stephen did."

Suddenly she stood on her toes, leaning forward, resting her hands on my chest, and kissed me softly but firmly on the lips. "If you're ever in Boston, that offer of a place to visit still stands." Throwing me a sly grin, she turned and ran lightly up the steps.

I had given Molly one of David's photocopies of the article and promised to destroy the others. So I walked down to the edge of water, carefully tore them into small pieces and dropped them into the surf. But the tide was going out, and they kept sticking in the sand. I had to run out in my bare feet and kick them into the water.

I stubbed my toe and began to swear. I swore at Stephen for convincing me not to tell the truth to Jessie, at David for being just another creep, at Jessie for believing in him and at myself for wanting to know too much and then being too much of a coward to tell it.

By the time I was done, the waves had washed the sand clean of paper. They didn't seem to be shocked by the news or to mind knowing the truth. Maybe that's because Jessie was right: the ocean is the one thing that never changes, and if you never change, then nothing can frighten you. I waved at the ocean and it waved back. Then I turned and headed up toward the cliffs.

\*     \*     \*     \*     \*